This book may be kept

FOURTEEN DAYS

A fine will be charged for each day the book is kept overtime.

FEB 6 '68			
Mrs. Williams			
Nicholas			
OCT 2 '69			
OCT 4 '68			
NOV			
0 '70			
JAN 1976			
GAYLORD 142			PRINTED IN U.S.A.

I, Roberta

I, Roberta

by

Elizabeth Gray Vining

J. B. LIPPINCOTT COMPANY

PHILADELPHIA & NEW YORK

23,573

For George Stevens,
editor and friend

I, Roberta

1

Four days have passed and I still see her sitting there in my parlor, holding Kent on her lap and hugging him to her cushiony bosom. Her round, smooth, peach-bloom cheeks were wet with her tears; she dried them by pressing them against my son's springy black curls with a gesture of tenderness that would have been unnatural for me at any time and impossible at that moment. I was dry-eyed myself, cold to my very marrow from the shock of what I had heard.

I seldom use the parlor now, just going in once a week to dust it and to wind the grandfather clock, and it has a faintly musty smell. Except for the flowered carpet and the book on the pie-crust table, there isn't anything in that room less than a hundred years old. Even the book, *The Republican Court: American Society in the Days of Washington*, was published in 1850. Father gave it to Mother when he was courting her; he said she looked like Mrs. Thomas Randolph; she did, too; even as a child I could see it. Most of the furniture was made for my great-grandmother Ewing by an itinerant cabinetmaker who had come up from Virginia soon after the Revolutionary War.

The sitting room behind the parlor was fragrant with the creeping arbutus that I had picked in the woods that morning and the library across the hall had the—to me —lovely odor of sunshine on books, but when she had appeared at the front door and handed me her visiting card with Mrs. Anthony Morelli on it and asked to see Mrs. Morelli, Senior, I invited her into the parlor.

"There isn't any Mrs. Anthony Morelli, Senior," I said. "I am Mrs. Anthony Morelli. Won't you sit down?"

"Oh," she said.

I could see that she was about to sink into the wing chair and I warned her hastily that it is not so soft as it looks: they did not put springs in them when that chair was made. She was in deep mourning, and her eyes, which must have been really a pretty, innocent blue, were pale and dull from weeping. But for all her smooth skin and round cheeks, her yellow hair, her general air of supposing herself young in spite of her widow's weeds, she wasn't actually, I was sure, much younger than I, if at all. I could tell by her hands. By the time a woman is thirty-seven, the skin on her hands has changed.

"Then our husbands must be—must have been— cousins," she said. "I just assumed that you would be Anthony's mother."

I was older than Tony, but not that much. Just five years. I accepted her suggestion that her husband had been Tony's cousin, but my heart had begun to thump. Had she brought me news of Tony after all this time?

I was curious, too, as to how she had got here. I don't mingle much with people in Ewingville, but I should know about any stranger in the village—and one named

10

Mrs. Anthony Morelli would have the whole place buzzing like an overturned beehive.

"Are you visiting somebody here?" I asked outright.

"I came down in the train from Camden."

The station, which is not really in the village, is a full mile from my house and the road is dusty, but there wasn't a speck on her neat little pointed black buttoned shoes. She must have come in the hack then. I wondered how much Ellwood had got out of her on the way over.

"You must be tired and thirsty. May I get you some refreshment?"

"Just a glass of cold water, thank you. I wouldn't refuse that."

Her voice and inflections were of Philadelphia and not first-chop Philadelphia either. I went out into the hall and through the dining room to the kitchen, where there is still a pump over the sink. The water in our well has iron in it, or else it is in the pipes from the well; anyhow I always keep a clean piece of cheesecloth tied over the mouth of the pump, and the water, after it had gushed a moment or two, was cold and pure. I would have offered her some of my home-made root beer but the keg was empty.

While I was pumping, Kent came into the room wearing his Fauntleroy suit which I had given him for Christmas. I had dressed him up because I had promised to take him to the new ice-cream parlor for a dish of ice cream.

"When are we going, Mama?"

"I don't know when we can go. I've got a visitor in the parlor. You run on upstairs and play with your soldiers till I call you."

"Can I see him?"

"*May* I see *her*—it's a lady. Not now. Maybe later. You trot along."

11

He looked so disappointed that I stopped pumping to get him a hermit from the cookie jar.

"I'll get rid of her as soon as I can," I promised.

Then I realized that the three o'clock must have gone and that there is no other up-train till five; I wondered if I could get her to say whatever she had to say quickly and then invite her to go along to the ice-cream parlor with us. I hate to break a promise to a child.

Kent went stamping up the back stairs and I started for the parlor with the glass of water and a plate of hermits on a tray. I noticed that my hand trembled just enough to slop the glass over a little, and I stopped to wipe up the drops and get a fringed napkin out of the sideboard drawer. It was thin with age and washing but I did not take the time to look for another. Then, knowing that just the name Anthony Morelli had been enough to make me tremble, I stood in the dim cool dining room, which has a greenish light because of the old box bushes outside the window, and counted ten.

I went back into the parlor and she drank the water. Then she told me who she was and that Tony had died. I told her who I was.

It was as if the earth had opened up at our feet between us, the way it is described as doing in lands where there are earthquakes, and we looked at each other aghast over the fissure. I felt as if it might snap shut again with both of us inside. Her face crumpled and she began to sob. I turned stiff and numb.

We were both Mrs. Anthony Morelli and it was the same man. Tony is dead. He died a month ago. I was married to him and she had thought she was. They had a fine wedding a year and a half ago and were living happily on North Broad Street in Philadelphia, until he went out one day without his rubbers and took cold and died of pneumonia within a week. She said that he died

12

reconciled with the Church—and just what had he told the priest? I wondered—and she "buried" him in the Holy Sepulchre Cemetery. They had no children. She had grieved over that, but now. . . . The tears flowed again.

At that moment Kent burst into the room demanding in a rather whining voice to know when we were going.

She looked at him, startled, and then suddenly, to my amazement, she opened wide her arms. He went into them and she gathered him up on her lap. Kent is a beautiful child. He has his father's looks and my reserve —he doesn't usually take to strangers, but he took to her. I let him stay there, since it seemed to be a comfort to her to hold him, but the numbness in me was beginning to wear off. I wanted desperately to be alone and I felt I could not stand having her here much longer.

"Why did you come here?" I asked her. "How did you know about me?"

"I was going through Anthony's things and I found a little piece of paper with his handwriting on it." She fumbled in her stiff new black handbag and brought it out, a yellowed slip of poor-quality paper all but worn through at the folds. "It was stuck in the lining of his wallet."

I opened it up. It was Tony's handwriting, there was no question of that. Handwriting, I often think, brings a person freshly to mind faster than anything else, even a photograph. It was a too-fancy hand but it had a kind of dash about it that was characteristic of him. "*Mrs. Anthony Morelli. Anthony Morelli, Jr. Ewingville, New Jersey.*" Tony must have written this when the baby was first born, put it inside his wallet and forgotten about it.

My married name is Morelli, my maiden name, Dobson; Mother was born a Ewing. Ever since the first Ewing

13

came to South Jersey on the ship *Kent* in 1680 there has been a Kent Ewing in every generation until first Mother and then I came, only children and girls. After Tony left me and we finally knew that he would not come back, Mother persuaded me to change Anthony Junior's name to Kent. I have never thought that Kent Ewing Morelli sounded as well as Anthony Morelli, Jr. —it is too patently a hybrid—but Mother wanted it so much and felt it so deeply that I went to the courthouse and had it done.

"I thought of course you were his mother, and I was so anxious to see you—her—and talk about Anthony that I couldn't wait to write you. I just put on my things and came on the first train I could get."

Hadn't it even occurred to her to wonder why he had never told her he had a mother living within twenty-five miles of North Broad Street? What *had* he told her anyhow? But she was soft, I thought, soft and unsuspecting and impulsive; past, like me, her youth.

Kent, who is usually as undemonstrative as a tadpole, suddenly hugged her and said, "I like you. I wish you was my mama."

Children will do that and it doesn't mean a thing, but I wished he had not just then.

Casting a quick look at me, half scared, half triumphant, she lowered her eyes and scrabbled in her handbag for a chocolate bud covered in silver foil, which she gave to him, saying warmly,

"So do I, darling. Run outdoors now and play while your mama and I talk."

It wasn't for her to send him off, but no matter.

"Go and find Pete," I said, "and tell him I want to speak to him right away."

I wanted no more talk. I had had all I could bear. I wanted only to be sure that she caught the five o'clock back to the city. Kent was too young to send to the livery stable for Ellwood but he could be trusted to find Pete Snaith next door.

"He's adorable," she said as soon as the door closed on his small, straight, black-velvet back. Almost every little boy you see, who's anything of a pet in the family, has a Little Lord Fauntleroy suit, and Kent does not look any more like the famous Birch drawings than most of them do. His legs, which are sturdy, wore ribbed white cotton stockings instead of black silk, and no golden ringlets hung down over his wide, lace-edged collar. But he is beautiful enough just the same to make strangers turn in the street to look at him a second time. His black shining hair curls all over his head, his eyes are large, dark, liquid Italian eyes, and his smooth child's skin is tinged with olive. Mother and I could never see any trace in him of Ewing or Dobson, except that his front teeth, like mine, have a little space between them. That—and of course his brains. He showed marked intelligence even as a baby. Mother maintained that he was potentially another Judge Ewing, but I can't imagine anybody named Morelli on the bench, not in South Jersey anyhow.

She—her name is Grace and I must stop calling her *she*. *She* is the devil's grandmother, Mother used to say when I offended—Grace Peacock, who had thought she was Mrs. Anthony Morelli, dabbed at her eyes again with her fine black-edged handkerchief, drew a long quavery breath and said in a loud voice,

"I want you to let me take him. I want to adopt him."

I just looked at her.

"He likes me. You could see that for yourself. I love children, and usually they take to me. I can do more for him than you can, living in the city and all. I would give him everything—school, college, travel. And love."

I have never since I was a child and fought with the neighborhood children wanted to hit anyone, but I wanted at that moment to hit her. I would have liked to strike her right across her soft pink face.

"I think you must be out of your mind," I said at last. Somewhere I found the strength not to order her out of the house. But absurd and outrageous as she was, I could not help pitying her too, even in a way feeling a kind of admiration for her. A month ago she had lost her husband by death and minutes ago lost him even more shockingly for a second time. Yet here she was, a creature evidently who lived, however shallowly, on love, clutching at the element that was life to her. That it was my child she wanted was apparently not in the least peculiar in her eyes.

"There are hundreds of other children to adopt," I said. "Children who need adopting."

"He was Anthony's child. He is the image of Anthony."

"Tony was a liar, a thief and a bigamist." It was bitter and brutal but it was the truth and I hate sentimentality. I did not say *deserter* to her, but he was that, too.

Her eyes filled again. "But he wasn't. You didn't know him. Or if he was, he had changed. When he knew real, deep love, his whole character responded. You couldn't have known him as I knew him. Are you a Catholic?"

"If you mean a Roman Catholic, no." I used to say the Creed, "I believe in the Holy Catholic Church," but it was the Episcopal Church, of course. She said Tony had died reconciled with the Church. He couldn't have told them everything but she did not know that, not at the time. Even now she probably thought his marriage to me didn't count, that hers did. She probably thought she would save Kent's soul as well as adopt an adorable child.

"You couldn't have known him as I knew him," she repeated.

"No doubt. But Kent is the son of the Tony who married me."

"If you really loved Kent—"

"No," I said. I meant, No, she could not have him.

We sat and looked at each other in hostile silence until Pete came to the front door. "You want me, Mrs. Morelli?" He was all patched elbows and bare feet. It is only the beginning of April but it was a warm day and he had already shed his shoes.

"Yes. Run over to the livery stable and tell Ellwood to bring his hack over in time to take this lady to the five o'clock."

She had followed me into the hall. "Oh, you needn't have troubled. I've already engaged the cab." She fumbled in the bag again and found a ten-cent piece for Pete. "Thank you for your trouble."

We still had twenty minutes to get through. I took her up to the bathroom, which Father had had made out of the old sewing room over the kitchen. The tub stands on a sort of platform in the middle of the room and the w.c. was put beside the window where he could enjoy a view of the garden. I could see her casting little appraising glances around as I led her upstairs, missing nothing, the old-fashioned furniture, the mended rug, the stain in the ceiling, the faded wallpaper, the antiquated bathroom. I could see that she was one of those city people who can't imagine anybody in the country having money or going abroad or having a library in the house. But she was right about the poverty. The money is gone and most of it went with Tony.

She probably can't imagine, either, a country person who knows that North Broad Street is a place where no one with any social knowledge would care to live. I have never gone beyond the Academy of the Fine Arts, but I imagine that the houses farther north are expensive and

new with cut-stone stables in back and marble lions at
the front steps. When I attended Miss Foote's School I
went back and forth to the city every day by train, ferry
and horsecar in good weather; in bad weather I could
stay overnight or longer with Mother's second cousin,
Cousin Alida French, who lived on Spruce Street. I
know the difference between north of Market and south
of Market. I know which side of Chestnut Street to walk
on, too.

By the time that Grace emerged from the bathroom,
her nose still pink under a coating of white complexion
powder, Ellwood was already waiting in the driveway.
His whole body, usually as limp as a jointed doll whose
inner elastic has stretched, was for once alert, with
curiosity, no doubt. Even his old nag looked livelier than
usual.

Kent came round the corner of the house in time to kiss
her good-by and be told to call her "Auntie Grace,"
which Ellwood heard, and Pete too, who was clipping
the hedge between the houses with remarkable industry.

We shook hands formally.

"I really meant it," she said in a lowered voice, "but
we'll let it rest for a while." She opened her mouth to say
something further, shut it, then decided to say it after
all. "There's more to me than you think. I can see you're
a *good* woman, and you've had a blow—and so have I,
God knows. We'll let it rest for a while until we both
know our minds better."

I could see that she was shrewder than I had given
her credit for. And I could see that she was one of those
people who have always had whatever they wanted and
expected to go on having it.

I couldn't sleep that night, or the next one. I was
seething with emotions that I couldn't untangle. And if

18

the word *seething* is hackneyed, it is still what I mean. I looked it up in the dictionary, and one definition is "to be in a state of inner turmoil, agitation or ferment." Anger, pain, resentment, grief—yes, grief for Tony who is dead and now can never come back as I sometimes dreamed he would, to be received with contempt or forgiveness, according to the color of my daydream at the moment—humiliation, pity, horror—for isn't bigamy one of the meanest betrayals?—all agitated and fermented in the turmoil within me.

Sometimes out of the welter of pictures, past and present, that poured through my mind, I saw her sitting with Kent in her lap, saw him turn to hug her and say, "I wish you was my mama." He was cross with me because I had failed on the promised trip to the ice-cream parlor, but I couldn't help wondering if there was more to it than that. I was so determined, after Mother died and there were just the two of us, not to live on him or let my need suck his life dry, that perhaps I had overdone it. Perhaps he had craved more openly expressed affection.

In the daytime I went about as usual, took Kent for the ice cream, worked in the garden cleaning up after the winter, raking leaves and burning them. I was relieved to find that Grace had told Ellwood nothing. Esther Snaith came over from next door on the pretext of borrowing a cup of sugar and asked outright who my visitor from Philadelphia was. I was put to it to answer.

"I don't often see any of Cousin Alida French's friends any more," I said. "It was a great surprise." It was not very adroit. I don't like to lie.

"Funny her coming so suddenly, wasn't it. She must have had something pressing to talk about with you."

I let that fall and roll away. With some asperity she thanked me for the sugar and went off, every angle of her thin body and her stiff walk eloquent of offense taken.

I read to Kent and fixed his marble run, a toy left over from my own childhood. I think Father made it, a narrow wooden track on which marbles ran down hill and around curves, getting up momentum enough to roll out over the carpet at the end, the one that went the farthest winning. Kent had some kind of imaginative game with it—the red marble was the favorite—which he played with silent, secret absorption. The days were bearable, being about the same as usual, but the nights have been torture.

On the third night a sentence flashed through my mind: "The unexamined life is not worth living." It was Socrates who said it, I know that, but where did he say it? In what context? I got up and lit my bedside candle and went down into the library to see if I could find it. Grandfather Ewing would have placed it in a minute and in Greek too. Fortunately he also had Plato in English.

The stairs creaked as I went down, clutching my old gray wrapper tight around me. It is nothing unusual for me to go down to find a book at night. Mother and I used to sit up reading till after midnight and then sleep late in the morning, to the scandal of the neighbors, who thought there was something immoral about so much reading and not keeping regular hours. The library is as old as the house and most of the books are old, though Father added some books on insurance and the usual popular novels and Mother and I bought books as long as we could afford to.

I couldn't find it, riffling through the *Phaedo* and the *Symposium*. "Know thyself," I learned from Bartlett's *Familiar Quotations*, comes from the Delphic Oracle and it's not exactly the same anyhow.

20

But how much did I know of myself? I thought, sitting down in Father's unsightly but comfortable stationary rocker. As to my life, I had brooded about it, resented it, endured it and sometimes enjoyed it, but I had never examined it. Nor ever controlled it, either. I had been like a log floating down a stream, nudged by the bank on this side, then on that, banging against a rock or borne smoothly along by the water when it flowed swiftly, but never deciding its own direction.

The room was cold. After the unseasonably warm spell, the wind had risen and was driving a sleety rain against the shutters. I went back upstairs to bed, still thinking about my unexamined life.

Who am I, anyhow? The daughter of Robert Dobson and Caroline Ewing Dobson. The wife of Tony Morelli. The widow of Tony Morelli. The mother of Kent Morelli. Roberta Ewing Dobson Morelli. Names. A chair has names. Wing, rocker, *chaise*, *Lehnstuhl* and the rest. But what do they tell of the essential *chair*ishness of it, the way it feels receiving a tired body or having a tense one perch on its edge or standing for days neglected, always ready and never used?

Who am I? The *me* of me, what is it?

And so, I thought, I will examine my life and find out. Every evening after Kent is in bed, instead of reading myself to sleep as usual, I will stoke the stove in the sitting room and sit at the desk and write whatever comes into my head. Beginning with Grace's visit.

I have written this on April 6th, 1895. My fingers are stiff and the fire has gone out, but there's not much use in going to bed now at all. The sky is already gray.

2

At least I have a pretty fair idea of what other people think of me. They show it by the things they say to me and don't say to me; by what they say to other people, who repeat it, perhaps with embellishments or omissions, to me; by the expressions on their faces. I am observant. Mother used to say quite often that she thought I was more of an observer of life than a partaker in it, and no doubt that is true, though it seems to me that at times I have partaken of larger and more bitter gulps of it than most of the people whom I watch.

She—Grace—thought I was *good*, by which she probably meant what most people mean by *good:* biddable, amenable to their direction. She also thought I underestimated her, and so I did, at first; she is a type that I have not come into contact with before.

At Miss Foote's they thought I was intelligent and homely and not easy to know; in fact not very much worth knowing, since I emerged from South Jersey and went back to it, and South Jersey they thought of as some kind of social wilderness that you traversed in order to get to Cape May, if you spent the summer there instead of Jamestown or the Poconos.

Mother thought of me as an extension of herself and her father, Judge Ewing, and therefore not only essential to her but superior to the ordinary run of people. There was much more to it than that, but that was what turned the village against us. There is nothing you can do that so infuriates a country town as to think you are better than other people. If you compound it by a sensational marriage to a foreigner, by being deserted and by losing your money, you become first ridiculous and then contemptible in their eyes.

I am skipping over too much. Am I, after all, a person who cannot write, even to herself, the truth as she knows it? When I married Tony, who had been our hired man, the village was excited and curious; they decided that I was more attractive than they had thought. When the baby came too early, they found me sensual—and liked me a little better for it. When Mother died, I think they pitied me. But the worst thing you can do in a village like ours is to lose your money. That is fatal.

Tony? He thought I was a gullible old maid.

Father loved me, but he could not compete with Mother, and he died when I was sixteen.

What Ned Wadsworth thought of me I don't know, really. I never did.

April 7th

3

The last time I saw Ned really to talk to was nearly three years ago, soon after Mother's death. It was a very hot, sticky day in August and he came in his shirt sleeves. The shirt was immaculate and he wore a stiff collar and tie, but I confess I was taken aback by his not wearing his coat for a visit of condolence.

I took him into the sitting room and he prowled about a bit before he sat down, looking at the things on the table and the mantel, turning the little green china temple dog over in his hands. He is a tall man, quick and lithe in movement, slow and gentle of speech; light-haired with gray eyes behind steel-rimmed spectacles; not at all handsome but somehow very nice-looking. Probably it is his expression that attracts, for his face is full of kindness and candor, with a touch of quiet humor.

"I'm sorry about thy mother, Roberta," he said in his unexpectedly high, rather squeaky voice, which Mother used to mimic to perfection.

24

Ned is a Quaker. Some Quakers have a way, which I dislike, of saying *thee* to other Quakers and *you* to outsiders. If there's a roomful of Friends and non-Friends, they'll sort it out as quick as lightning, *thee*ing the sheep and *you*ing the goats in the same breath. But Ned always *thee*'s everybody.

"She was a fine woman," he went on in his leisurely way. "She hadn't any use for me at all, but I always liked her. She knew her own mind. I like that in people."

As I look back I think I did not notice this particularly at the time, though I noticed it enough to remember it, but now it strikes me as if freshly said, for what am I doing every night late in the sitting room at my desk but trying to learn my own mind?

He said some other things about her which I have forgotten, and then he put his fingers in his collar and eased his neck before he went on.

"It's hard on thee in every way. I suppose thee realizes that her annuity will stop now?"

I realized it very well. It had been forming a considerable part of our income, though it was only a small annuity which Grandfather had bought her as a wedding present so that she would always have money which was wholly her own to do what she liked with. Ned knew about it because he was now head of the insurance agency through which it had come.

I nodded.

"I supposed thee did. I didn't come to tell thee about that but about something else. Earl Elder would like to give up the post office."

Ever since I could remember, the Ewingville Post Office had occupied one corner of Elder's General Store; it was Earl Junior who was running it now. I couldn't see that this had anything to do with me but I replied with a show of interest, "Would he? It won't seem natural not to go there for the mail." Not that I ever had much mail to speak of.

"I thought that perhaps thee might like to take it," said Ned abruptly. "Thee could use that room to the left of thy front door. It would be quite easy to make one of those windows on the driveway into a door. Then people wouldn't have to go into thy house—the living part of it—at all. Thee would have the rent for the room as well as the salary and together they would make up what you had from the annuity."

Turn my library—and not only mine but my grandfather's and my son's, too—into a common post office where any Tom, Dick and Harry could come in at will? Replace the bookshelves with rows of mailboxes and the chairs and big mahogany table with high wooden counters with holes for inkwells solid with old ink—and a spittoon in the corner? Stand behind a little iron grill myself and sell penny postcards to all and sundry? I tried to hide my feeling of outrage at the suggestion. In fact, it makes me hot even now. But I knew it was good of Ned, who besides being insurance agent and notary public and seller of real estate had a finger in nearly every other pie in the region, to trouble himself about my affairs. I tried to appear grateful.

"Thank you," I said stiffly, "but I couldn't think of it."

He unfolded himself from the too-small chair that he had elected to sit in and stood looking down at me with a little smile.

"No, I can see thee can't. Well, I wish thee well, Roberta."

After I had seen him out I came back to the sitting room and prowled around it as he had done, looking at the things on the mantel, the green china temple dog from Peking which had attracted Ned's attention, the

26

photograph of Mother taken sideways to show her bustle, the gilt clock and the two alabaster vases full of pampas grass, and the center table with its green and yellow glass-shaded lamp and green serge tablecloth, the piles of books and my sewing basket.

He married another Quaker, Anna Chase—Mother said she had *chased* him—and they have four children. They live in the old Wadsworth house across the street from the Friends Meeting at the west end of Main Street.

April 8th

4

The first Ewing to come to this country was Thomas Ewing, yeoman, of Bugbrooke, Northamptonshire. He was a Quaker, but he had all his children who were born in England baptized just the same, possibly in an excess of caution. He was land hungry, I gather, and I think the Quaker land in New Jersey tempted him. He got three thousand acres of it and settled in 1680 on the old Ewing place outside the village, which is now rented to a French-Canadian family. The "new" part of the house was built in 1767, of brick laid in Flemish bond, with the name and the date picked out in blue bricks on the gable end of the house. The old part became a dining room and kitchen wing with an attic above. My tenants have two hundred acres to farm—they raise wheat and hay and hops and garden vegetables—and I have this house in the village, which was settled by Thomas Ewing's sons. The house was built in 1787 by Kent Ewing, my great-grandfather, who made a fortune for those days in glass. It was—and still is—the show place of the village, with its fan doorway and double chimneys at both ends. It is built of white limestone, which was all quarried out of this region by 1800, so that you can pretty well date any stone house hereabouts. In the beginning it stood on the edge of the village in the middle of five or six acres, but they have been sold bit by bit and now the lot is one hundred feet wide and three hundred feet deep. The Snaith house next door, an ugly frame affair painted in shades of buff and chocolate, is only partly hidden by the privet hedge between us.

Some of the original Thomas's descendants went to Philadelphia and prospered and, marrying daughters of Cadwalladers and Morrises and Woods, shrugged off their South Jersey origin. Others later went west and prospered or did not prosper; in either case they were seen no more, except for occasional distant cousins who appeared in Ewingville in my childhood, declared that the East was grimy and unfriendly, and enthusiastically went back to Kansas or Iowa or wherever it was they came from.

The Ewings did not long remain Quakers. In the early 1690's the Society of Friends was torn by one of the earliest of the schisms that from time to time have rent it; this was the Keithian Controversy, headed by a man named George Keith, who wrote books called *The Fundamental Truths of Christianity* and *Truth and Innocency Defended against Calumny and Defamation*, which I have in the library but have never read. When he was thrown out of the fold he joined the Church of England and was ordained; he then became a member of the Society for the Propagation of the Gospel and came back to America as a missionary to those who had ejected him. In 1704 Thomas Ewing, who can scarcely

29

have been a very ardent Quaker anyhow, and all his family became Episcopalians and helped to found the little Episcopal church, also built of limestone, in the village. It was named St. Thomas's and I have always wondered about that.

There are not many Quakers in the village now; they use only half of their old meetinghouse at the other end of town from my house. They keep pretty much to themselves, maintaining a small school for their young children and mostly sending the older ones to George School, a Quaker boarding school in Pennsylvania. Fewer and fewer of them come back and the meeting dwindles. Not many of them wear the plain dress now— gray gowns and bonnets—but all of them are dowdy and wear sober colors. But they are respected in the village; none of them seem to be poor.

If there are few Quakers in Ewingville now, there are even fewer Episcopalians. Even when dear old Dr. Herbert was alive and my family was in a position to support it, St. Thomas's lost members every year, mostly by death. Now it is reduced to being a mission church with only occasional services, which I never attend.

The Methodist church is the largest as well as the newest, but many of the village people are nothing at all. The handful of R.C.'s go to Exeter, the county seat, to Mass. Tony, who was born, he said, a Protestant, had been converted to Catholicism by the time I knew him, but as he was a lapsed one, he didn't bother.

April 9th

5

We have all been reading people, to whom books are the bread of life. Every generation has left its deposit of books in the library. The second—or was it the third?—Thomas was passionately interested in plays. He used to go up to Philadelphia to the Southwark Theater, even though it was a day's trip each way then and he had to stay overnight. He brought in Shakespeare and Congreve and Sheridan and such forgotten dramatists as Thomas Godfrey and Royall Tyler. Kent the glassmaker went in for natural history; he bought Linnaeus and Bartram and Wilson and Audubon, with beautiful pictures that I used to pore over as a child. The old judge was a classicist. The Dickens, Scott, Thackeray, Charles Brockden Brown and most of the rest of the novels I owe to Father. Mother liked history and philosophy and also little pious books like *The Christian Year*, *Prayers Ancient and Modern*, *Day by Day* and so on.

Travel is my meat. Travel books are expensive and I

don't buy any now, but I reread the old ones, the guide-books and all. I plan trips. Sometimes I just go to the places I've been and settle down to enjoy them for as long as I like; other times I pick out new places and make lists of what I would go to see there.

Mother and I went abroad three times; the first time in 1880, when I was twenty-two and Ned Wadsworth was hanging about me; the second time in 1882 when he had been finally shaken off—that is to say, when he had married Anna Chase; and the last time in 1886, which was the time I enjoyed most. I didn't enjoy the trip in 1882 at all. We spent the whole time in Paris, and Mother used to scold me every day for "moping" and spoiling her pleasure. She was radiant. At forty-six she looked ten years younger, her violet eyes clear and bright, her skin smooth, not a trace of gray in her chest-nut hair and her chin line propped up by high collars. (I remember saying to her, despairingly, when I was seventeen or eighteen, "*Why* didn't you pass along your beauty to your only daughter?" I suppose I was hoping that she would say something comforting like, Oh, you're not so bad-looking, but she didn't. She just laughed a little and said lightly, "The plain features of the Dobsons would spoil any pretty woman's children." Another time, though, she did praise my nose. But this was much later, just a little before she died. She said it was much my best feature. Grateful though I was to have any feature that could be termed my best, even while I realized that in that context *best* is not as good as a simple *good*. I really did not particularly like my nose, which, though not large, is distinctly aquiline. But Mother went on to say that aquiline noses wear better and in the long run are more distinguished than re-troussé noses like hers. "Women as they get older," she said, "go soft, or go hard, or go fine. You with that nose of yours will go fine. I am going soft, I am afraid.")

That summer in Paris she was still beautiful. There was a man whom we met on the boat going over, a lawyer from Cincinnati, who was fascinated by her. He had been intending to travel through Italy but he stayed in Paris instead and came every day to take us about. He was a widower, and sometimes I wonder if she would have married him if I had not been there.

Still, even so, I would like to go back to Paris, to stay again at that pension on the left bank. Another time I would spend much less time in churches and much more in the Louvre. We brought back a stack of books on the history of Paris and the history of art, and now I would be better equipped to enjoy Paris. In 1886 we didn't go near it. We went through Holland to Heidelberg, where we stayed most of the summer, both of us studying German like mad and climbing up to the Castle every fine day.

Kent, too, is bookish. He is getting impatient with being read to and wants to tear the meaning out of the pages for himself. Two or three months ago he caught on to the fact that letters (which he had learned from his blocks) make words, and now if I sit down to sew for a little while, he is right there with his book, "wording" me.

"Mama, what does p-o-r-r-i-d-g-e spell? Oh. What does b-r-o-w-n-i-e spell? Oh." And so on as long as I am sitting still.

April 10

6

She said that day—Grace—"If you really loved Kent—" and I interrupted her with "No." I meant, No, you can't have him, but it might have sounded as if I meant, No, I don't love him. But she could not possibly have imagined that I meant that. Of course a mother loves her child, and especially a mother who has suffered as I have.

Or do I deceive myself? Was my love for him poisoned by the terror and revulsion with which I met the realization that I was pregnant? How does one know about oneself?

I had known, of course, that it was possible after that afternoon in Tony's little sitting room over the stable— which I'll have to write about later, if I can—but I kept hoping that somehow it would not happen to me. I ran up and down stairs furiously and I took deep, steaming, hot baths, but it was no use. I didn't tell Mother for nearly four months. Then on the same day that I first felt life stirring deep in the inner core of me, Mother suddenly said at the lunch table, "You're eating too much, Roberta. You're losing your waistline."

So it came out. Not at lunch, of course, for we still had a maid in the house, but afterwards in Mother's bedroom with the door shut and the July sun streaming onto the Marseilles counterpane on her big sleigh bed.

I knew it must be dreadful for Mother to hear me blurting out what had happened. My pain for her was woven into my anguish for myself. I got it all out in a single howl and then stood silent, with burning face and twisting fingers, waiting for whatever reproaches she should heap on my head.

I don't know what I expected her to do. I had read enough trashy novels to know that girls in such cases frequently were turned out into the snow. But I was not a girl—I was nearly thirty-two—and Mother had her pride. And of course she loved me. But she had also on occasion a very caustic tongue. What I hoped—and I had thought about it a great deal in those four months— was that we could go abroad for the fall and winter and I could have the baby in Paris or Rome or somewhere and leave it to be adopted. There was a girl at school who did that. It was not supposed to be known, of course, but it was whispered about.

Mother laughed.

It looks preposterous, shocking, written out like that. I feel almost disloyal to write it. It was gone the next moment and probably it was not really laughter, that little gurgle of apparent amusement, but only a physical reaction to shock. And yet I know that Mother did make enemies for herself occasionally by laughing at the wrong moment, by finding something ludicrous in situations that might have been expected to evoke sympathy or, in this case, anger or horror. But I shall never forget that moment. I was braced for a bitter accusation of immorality, of disgracing the family, and Mother laughed. I burst into tears.

She was serious the next moment and very practical. "You'll have to be married right away," she said briskly.

"Married? To Tony Morelli?" When Ned Wadsworth had not been good enough for me?

"He is handsome and charming—obviously—but even if he weren't you must see that you haven't any choice in the matter."

Haltingly I explained my idea of going to Europe.

"And just toss the baby on to the world? *Roberta!*"

She was really shocked. I knew her so well, all the small signs under her controlled surface, the strained tightness around her mouth that was always a sign of inner distress, the darkening of her eyes and the sudden wild look in them, her whitening knuckles.

"I—I thought somebody might adopt it."

"Who? How would you find them? How would you know how they would treat it?"

"I don't know," I said slowly, "whether Tony wants to marry me." It had been very easy to avoid him since that day.

"He'll have to. But I think he'll be willing enough. He's ambitious. And you've cared enough for each other to create a child between you. Now you've a duty to that child."

It was strange, but Mother really liked Tony. She believed his story about being born of a good family in Lombardy, the son of a priest who couldn't stand the R.C. Church after all, who broke his vows and left it and married, and who was so persecuted by his former parishioners that he died of consumption and his wife too, and Tony came to America to make his way in a new country, a country of opportunity and kind, beautiful women like Mother.

36

If Mother liked him, I loved him. It is hard to remember it now, but for a while I did. And Mother, who had accepted my sin and shame with such forbearance, such real goodness, I literally at that moment worshiped.

When Tony and I were married and the village got accustomed to it and the baby was born, thereby starting up a new forest fire of gossip, and the monthly nurse put that warm, heavy, squalling bundle of life in my arms, something came to birth in me different from anything else I have ever known, or imagined.

Oh, I loved Kent from the first. I love him more all the time as his personality develops.

I love him, but I worry about him. I wonder where the money is coming from to bring him up as a Ewing should be brought up.

April 11th

7

I should have felt a premonition this morning when Kent asked out of the blue, "When is Auntie Grace coming again?"

He had not mentioned her since she was here and I thought he had forgotten her.

"Oh, I don't suppose she'll come again at all. She never came before."

"Let's ask her. I liked her."

Poor mite. Most children have family and friends coming and going about their houses bringing life and warmth and a breath of air from the world beyond. Our house is dull and empty for a little boy of five. But I certainly do not want to fill it with Grace. To distract him I suggested,

"How would you like to go out to the farm and get roots for root beer?"

His face lit up and he said no more about his new auntie.

Like most people hereabouts I keep a keg of home-made root beer on hand. Most families have their own recipes handed down through the years; I think ours is much better than the one the Hireses down at Salem are using for the root beer that they bottle and sell so profitably.

I hard-boiled two brown eggs and made some sand-wiches for our lunch, put on my old green skirt and battered straw hat with the brim, and got Kent into his last year's sailor suit. I'd cut the tunic off and put elastic in the hem so that it made a full blouse above the straight little trousers. He looked very nice. We started out gaily, I carrying the lunch basket and Kent the basket for the roots.

It was a glorious spring morning, sunny and cool with puffy clouds moving across the deep blue sky. People say South Jersey is uninteresting because it is so flat, but where else—except the prairies, of course—can you see so much sky? I love our wide level fields sweeping to the horizon, with here and there a wood lot or a line of un-even cedars or a cluster of farm buildings, all dwarfed by the vast reaches of blue overhead.

We went past our stable and out the back gate into the alley, down the alley to Cook Street, which soon becomes the old road to Haines Corners. Meadow larks and redwings perched on the top bars of snake fences, and high above us a kingbird was harassing a crow.

"Will the lady at the farm give us buttermilk and ginger cookies again?"

"Perhaps, but you mustn't hint. What kind of roots do we look for?"

"Sassafras and spice bush—"

"Yes, and what else?"

"I don't know." He ran ahead on the sandy road.

It is a full two and a half miles to the farm and I

might have taken my wheel, but Kent is already a good walker. We met nobody at all for the first half hour. They were plowing in the Hitchcocks' forty-acre; old Mr. Hitchcock saw us and waved. Kent ran back to me.

"I want to go look at the horses," he said.

"No, let's go on now. You can see the horses at the farm."

A farmer I did not know came rattling toward us with an empty wagon, and we stood aside in the grass until the dust had settled from his passing.

"Is that a Patchen horse, Mama?"

"Goodness, no. Nothing special at all, just raw-boned." But where had he heard about Patchen horses? Certainly not from me.

Our farmhouse stands at the end of a long lane lined with cedars. Kent saw it in the distance and pointed it out to me, the brick house under a great red maple, the barn and stable and crib house, the circle of white pines on a little mound, where we always eat our lunch.

We have had the same tenants for about thirty years, a family named Duchamps from the Province of Quebec, who had found farming in New Hampshire too hard and answered the advertisement that Father had run in the *Farm Journal*. The sons are grown now and they want to buy the farm, which poses a problem for me. If I refuse to sell, they might look elsewhere and I don't want to lose them. On the other hand I don't want to sell the farm; it is the last bit of the original Thomas's three thousand acres.

We went directly to the house to speak to Mrs. Duchamps and tell her we were going to the wood lot for roots. She came to the back door with a flat iron in her hand.

"Can we see where the Indians had breakfast?" demanded Kent.

"*May* we. But I am afraid Mrs. Duchamps is busy."

Mrs. Duchamps, short, dark, plump, smiling, stood aside and waved us in. " 'E love that story," she said.

The big kitchen smelled of fresh bread and hot linen and beeswax. An iron cookstove had been put across the old hearth where once there had been cranes and blackened pots and long iron forks. A clotheshorse and all the chairs were draped with tablecloths and towels and men's shirts "hardening" after being ironed. There were geraniums on the window sills, blue crockery on open shelves and a little stoup of holy water on one wall.

"Tell about the Indians, Mama."

"In the old days," I told him the old story again as it had been told to me, "when your great-great-I-don't-know-how-many-greats-grandfather lived here, there were still Indians in the woods round about. They were friendly Indians because the settlers had treated them well. And always in this kitchen breakfast was kept for them. Often an Indian would drop in, eat his breakfast without a word, grunt his thanks, and go out again."

"What would he eat?"

"Corn meal mush, I expect, perhaps with molasses on it."

"And buttermilk?" With an innocent, wholly beguiling, sidelong glance at Mrs. Duchamps, who gave a delighted chuckle and put down her iron.

"Maybe *this* little Indian would like some buttermilk, *hein*?"

So he had a glassful and thrust his hand deep into a stone crock of ginger cookies, while Mrs. Duchamps caught us up with the news. There was a new family of baby pigs and six kittens with their eyes still shut and, Kent must guess what, yes, a *colt* over in the field.

I would have liked to see the colt myself—the Duchamps have a fine pair of Morgans—but I thought it was good for Kent to go off on his own. Some of the men were sure to be about the barn anyhow, and he couldn't get into any trouble. So he ran off and I made my way past the pines to the wood lot, to dig my sassafras, spicewood and black alder roots and to pick the thick, shiny green teaberry leaves in the open places where trees have been cut out. I bit one and enjoyed its spicy aromatic taste. In some places they are called checkerberries or winter-green, but we call them teaberries. Perhaps they used them to make tea during the Revolution, which does not seem very far past in this part of the country where "Hessian" is still the worst epithet you can use for some-one you don't like. It was very quiet and peaceful in the woods and I worked contentedly till Kent came clatter-ing up to say everybody had gone to dinner and he was hungry.

We ate our lunch as usual sitting on pine needles under the trees, and one of the Duchamps boys brought out glasses and more buttermilk. Kent talked about nothing but the new foal. "It's a filly, Mama, and her name is Dusty. She likes me to stroke her nose."

After we had finished eating, Mr. Duchamps, who had evidently been hovering about waiting to see me but not wanting to disturb our meal, came up with a brick in his hand.

"I 'ate to bother you, Mis' Morelli," he said apologeti-cally, "but I wish you'd come look at the chimley in the new part. This brick fell off it and I think the 'ole thing need repointing."

My heart sank. I knew before I looked at it that it did indeed need repointing; it needed it last year but I had postponed the evil day.

"I'll get estimates at once," I assured him. Father taught me that; it gives one time and sounds business-like.

We walked home more slowly and less lightheartedly

42

than we had come. At first Kent wore the empty lunch basket upside down on his head; later he handed it over to me to carry. He lagged behind, scuffing up the dust, obviously depressed over leaving the farm and the colt.

When we reached home at last, we found the Adams Express wagon in the driveway, a man just turning away from the kitchen door on which he had been fruitlessly pounding.

"I've got a big package for the little feller," he shouted.

Kent, receiving an infusion of new life, ran up from behind me and got there first.

"For me?" he cried incredulously.

"Are you Master Kent Morelli?"

The belated premonition struck now, but there was nothing to be done. The fat was in the fire. Master Kent Morelli was watching in open-mouthed delight while they unloaded a large—an enormous—crate and proceeded to whack it apart with expertly casual blows of a hammer.

Meanwhile a sheaf of papers on which PREPAID was printed in large black letters was handed to me to receipt. *From Mrs. Grace Morelli, North Broad Street, Philadelphia.* Like an automaton I signed, while before my eyes a large and expensive rocking horse emerged from the crate.

It was as big as a small pony; it had a flowing mane of real horsehair, a red saddle and leather stirrups; it was dappled gray and under its prancing feet were generously up-curving wooden rockers painted red. I could see just how it was going to be. The thing would move as it rocked, crashing into the furniture, battering against me. But the material damage was as nothing compared to the effect it was already having on Kent.

He was speechless, but his eyes were the eyes of one who has seen the beatific vision.

"Shall I put you on it?" said one of the men, making ready to take him under the arms and lift him up.

Kent pushed the man aside impatiently. "No, I can do it." He put one foot in the stirrup, flung the other leg over the horse's back as if he had been born to it, settled himself carefully in the saddle and began to rock.

The Adams Express men departed, after neatly stacking the wood from the crate beside the driveway. I have come in here and written this to calm myself. Kent is still rocking. What can I write to her? What am I going to do? Oh, she has got me at a disadvantage!

April 12th

8

I have been nearly driven mad by this horse. Kent is obsessed with it. He thinks of nothing else; it is his first thought in the morning and his last at night.

The stable has been locked up these last three years, but Kent has badgered me into opening it again. He keeps the horse in Black Jack's old stall. In the morning he feeds and waters this monstrous toy and grooms it with an old hairbrush he has begged from me; hour after hour in the day he rides it over the grass; at night he feeds it again and puts it to bed in the stable, carefully fastening the door and lovingly calling good night as I drag him off to his own bed.

He has named the wretched thing Auntie Grace and nothing I can say will budge him. Why not Dusty, I say persuasively, for the filly at the farm? Or Lookout, for the horse that won the Derby? Or Dapple Gray, for the horse in the nursery rhyme and because it is descriptive? I might be spitting into the wind. Its name is Auntie Grace.

That is not a name for a horse, I point out. It is a person's name. It simply sounds ridiculous. People will laugh at him. He sets his jaw and says nothing but later he tells me, doggedly and ostentatiously, that Auntie Grace is tired now and he is giving her a little rest.

"It's not a mare," I tell him wildly, "it's a stallion. No one in his senses would name a stallion Grace."

Solemnly he makes an investigation. "You can't tell," he reports austerely, and accurately.

Yesterday I lost my head and did a silly thing. "I *forbid* you to call it Auntie Grace," I cried.

His face turned dark. Rage and hate flashed out of his black eyes. For a moment he was not a little South Jersey boy at all; he was an Italian in a fury. His small nose, I saw, would some day be a formidable Roman nose, and foreigners long before his father had set their mark on his chin. "It's *my* horse!" he shouted.

With an effort I shrugged my shoulders. "Call it what you want," I said with belated indifference. I can only hope that he will in time forget it or that the other children will laugh him out of it.

But there are no other children that he plays with. Pete came over to look at the monster and to try to find out where it came from, but he soon lost interest.

It is borne in upon me that Kent has been starved for amusement. He has had the marble run, the old blocks, his lead soldiers—and not very many of them—a sandbox from which the sand is almost gone. My presents to him at birthdays and Christmas have been books and clothes. But even if I had been perceptive enough, and human enough, to realize what a little boy craved and needed, I could not have afforded to buy such a plaything as this.

It has taken me all week to concoct a letter to her. Even to begin it raised a problem with echoes of meaning. *Dear Grace?* I call her Grace to myself but I am not on first-name terms with her. We are not friends—or relatives. I suppose we might be termed wives-in-law, if she were not outside the law. *Dear Mrs. Morelli?* She was not Mrs. Morelli, and to call her that implies that I accept something which I do not accept. *Dear Auntie Grace?* But this has a false playfulness about it and moreover it tacitly approves the relationship entered into by her and Kent without my acquiescence.

So I begin it, choosing the least of the three evils, *Dear Mrs. Morelli.* And I have to acknowledge that she has tactfully stopped calling herself Mrs. Anthony Morelli. The receipt I signed designated the sender as Mrs. Grace Morelli.

It is far too handsome and extravagant a present. If I could have done so before Kent saw it I would have returned it to you as something more expensive than I was willing to accept, but he was on hand when it arrived.

I could not bring myself to say that it was kind of her or even that I knew she meant well, for I did not. I was sure she was not motivated by kindness alone; she wanted to engage Kent's affection and undermine his love of me. I gritted my teeth and wrote the truth I thought she was entitled to along with the other truths:

I cannot conceal from you that Kent is wild with delight and loves the toy to distraction. But please do not send anything more. I hope you will understand how I feel. Very sincerely yours, Roberta Ewing Morelli.

I took it to the post office, which is still in Elder's store, and mailed it this morning.

Seeing the stable open again, being dragged into it by Kent to admire some new arrangement he has made for the comfort and well-being of his steed, has brought memories crowding.

47

Grandfather kept a pair of fast Patchen horses there and every morning he drove the five miles to the county seat; every afternoon, late, he came trotting smartly back again. People set their watches by him.

Mother hated those horses and lived in deathly fear of them. She told me once that Grandmother, who died before I was born, felt the same way about them. The original Patchen horse was a famous harness racer named Tom Patchen, and the strain, which was very popular in this part of the country, was bred from him. They were smart-looking, very fast, and had strength and stamina, but they were often vicious and always difficult to control. Grandfather took pride in his ability to handle his pair.

After his death one of the pair—was its name Black Star?—was sold and Father kept Black Jack. We had a couple living in the rooms over the carriage house then, Dennis, who took care of Black Jack and the garden, and his wife, Kate, who was our cook; then there was a chambermaid who doubled as waitress.

We had a buggy and a carriage, but neither was used very much. Father took the buggy when he had an errand to do in Exeter; sometimes Dennis drove Mother and me out to the farm in the carriage. Or we all went out for a Sunday afternoon ride. But Black Jack never had enough exercise and he was always so fresh that Mother and I on the back seat were in a state of alarm throughout the drive. He would shy at a piece of paper, and a boy with a fishing pole over his shoulder would have him on his hind legs, while Mother uttered little squeals of terror and I clutched the upright tensely. If you ever offered him a carrot or a lump of sugar he tried to bite you.

Mother used to beg Father to sell Black Jack. We didn't need him, she used to plead. Father walked to work, which was the same work that Ned Wadsworth now does in the same office. If we went any distance we took the train. If we wanted just a ride in the country we could always hire something quieter from the livery stable.

I was sixteen and a junior at Miss Foote's when Black Jack ran away with Father.

It was a mild russet and violet November day with pale sunshine and misty distances. I was coming home from school as usual, plodding along the road from the station with a load of books on my arm. When I crossed Main Street I saw people standing in little knots, talking; they fell silent when I passed and looked at me as if they wanted to speak but did not dare. It made me vaguely uncomfortable, but I was wrapped in the daydream that occupied my trips back and forth from the city and insulated me almost entirely from reality at that time, and though I saw people talking and looking at me, distressed and uncertain, I was not in any immediate way conscious of them. I went on home impervious. Even when I saw that something had struck against the gatepost, breaking off a piece of it and leaving a patch of raw splintered wood, I was not alarmed.

As soon as I opened the front door, which was always on the deadlatch in easy country fashion, I met the full impact of the tragedy, of which a girl who was more alert than I might have received a dozen subtle warnings along the way from the station.

The hall seemed swarming with people, the doctor, some men I did not know, Mother struggling in the awkward arms of a sympathetic neighbor. Father lay stretched motionless on a door propped on two chairs, his head bloody, his face gray, his pince-nez on their black ribbon dangling broken.

When Mother saw me she cried, "Don't look!" and,

49

breaking away from the neighbor, drew me into the library, where we cradled each other in our arms and cried together. When she could speak she told me what had happened.

Black Jack had bolted, as she had always known he would, and Father had been thrown out of the buggy, falling on his head against the Martins' mounting block. Black Jack came home first with the buggy careening behind him, banging against the gatepost. It took longer for the Martins, who were first on the scene, to get the doctor and then two men with a door to use for a stretcher to carry Father home. He was dead before the doctor got there. He could not have suffered; perhaps he never knew what happened.

It was Mother I thought of at the time, not Father. Mother who had suffered such shock and grief, who had hated the horse and had always known something like this would happen though Father would never listen to her, Mother who was so brave and broken, such a beautiful young widow, Mother who depended so on me. I never went back to Miss Foote's, not even to finish the term, for Mother needed me.

In this journey of discovery into myself, I should follow now the path marked Father, but every day in the stable and the carriage house it is Tony I am thinking of.

April 19th

9

I saw Tony for the first time on October 17th, 1888. I remember the date for it was my thirty-first birthday and I was feeling old and unwanted, unmarried, bored. The day itself was beautiful, as October 17th almost always is. I began to keep account of the weather on my birthday from the time I was eight, and it has only once rained during all these years and very seldom even been cloudy. That day was sparkling, with high wind-driven clouds scudding across a brilliant blue sky and the air full of the scarlet five-fingered leaves of the sweet gum. Mother had forgotten my birthday as she often did, even when I was a child. It was absurd of me to feel hurt at my age, but I did; so I tied a scarf around my head and went out into the garden to work it off raking leaves. Dennis and Kate were gone by that time. While we were in Germany two years earlier they had found work that paid better. We missed them. Delia took Kate's place fairly well, but we really needed a man about the house.

The casual by-the-day help we were able to get did not keep things looking as they used to look.

After I had got happily absorbed in raking leaves, Mother appeared at the window and crooked her finger at me to come to her. She wouldn't call to me out of a window, of course, and so I had to drop my rake and go all the way in, to be told that it was not necessary for me to do yard work, that she would send for old colored Moses. I said impatiently that I knew that but I wanted to do it.

She sighed and looked hurt. Her lower lip fell away a little from the upper one and stayed there, a signal familiar to me. She would be droopy and accusingly silent for the rest of the day.

"I'm sorry, Mother," I said hastily.

We loved each other but we had a hundred ways of hurting each other. A stranger—or for that matter a friend—if one were present might not even suspect that a poignant but almost silent battle was being fought under his very nose.

That time Mother decided to be indulgent. "Go ahead, if you want to, dear, of course," she said kindly. I went off, relieved but resentful, feeling that at thirty-one I had behaved like a child and that Mother had somehow maneuvered me into it.

But raking leaves and piling them in the driveway, where I set fire to them, raised my spirits. I watched the flames dart up through the curling leaves, draw together in a cone of fire that flared high then low in a gust of wind, as if curtseying. I stood leaning on my rake till they died down to fragrant smoke, trying to remember the poem I had learned as a child.

O suns and skies and clouds of June
And flowers of June together,

Ye cannot rival for one hour
October's bright blue weather.

Was it by Celia Thaxter? Or Helen Hunt Jackson?

By that time exhilarated, I decided that the grass needed a final mowing, went to the tool house and got out the lawn mower. It was a heavy old one, and I had not cut more than a swathe or two in the front lawn before I was stopping to puff and to mop my wet forehead with the back of my smoky hand. I had not heard anyone approach and I jumped when a voice behind me said:

"That's too hard work for you, Miss. I'd be glad to do it."

Startled, I whirled around. Later Tony used to say that seeing me from a distance, from the back, he had thought I was a young girl, but that the face I turned on him, streaked with sweat and smoke, was a witch's face.

What I saw was a young man who looked like the gondolier we had had in Venice eight years earlier: slender, dark, romantically handsome, wearing shabby black, with a low white collar, open at the throat, turned over his jacket.

"Oh, I couldn't," I demurred, confused.

"I'm looking for work," he said. He spoke with a slight accent, but his English was good. He did not look exactly like a workman but still not quite like a gentleman either. His voice was slow, soothing, yet with a faint touch of humor in it, as if he were amused—at himself or you?

"Oh, all right then. We pay Moses twenty cents an hour."

"Thank you, Miss." He smiled, a flash of white teeth in his olive-skinned face.

53

He peeled off his jacket and went to work without saying anything more. I stood watching him, rather uncertainly, feeling dismissed from his attention. In a few minutes he took off his white shirt and hung it carefully on the snowball bush. His shoulders were broad and his hips narrow; though he was not tall, he was well built and did not seem small. He wore a torn undershirt which was clean and looked very white against his dark skin. I watched him as he went up and down the lawn, back and forth, cutting even paths in the grass until, as he went past me, he flashed another brilliant smile, not exactly impudent but so full of awareness of himself and of me watching him that I turned hastily and went indoors.

Mother caught me in the hall. "Who is that, Roberta?"

"I don't know his name or anything about him. He said he was looking for work. We're paying him twenty cents an hour."

"I told you I'd get Moses."

"Yes, I know. But this man was here. He came up and offered. And evidently he needs the work."

"He doesn't look like a workman."

"Perhaps he's down on his luck."

"Where do you pick up such vulgar expressions? You look tired. Why don't you go lie down for a while? I'll take care of this man."

So I did not see him again that day.

At supper Mother told me that his name was Tony Morelli, that he was twenty-six, that he came from Italy and had been in this country for two years but had not been able to find steady work of the kind he wanted to do.

"What kind is that?"

"He said he wanted to be in business."

"He's certainly different from the Italians who are coming in to work on the farms down around Vineland."

"They are mostly from the south of Italy, I believe—Calabrians. This man is from Lombardy, he told me. He seemed proud of it. He has a good voice."

The next morning he appeared again and asked Mother if he could take the screens down for her. Later he washed the windows. The following day he cleaned the cellar. Delia gave him lunch in the kitchen and was loud in her praises of him. He was polite and easy-like, she said, and he was a good worker and didn't waste no time.

I went up to Philadelphia to spend the night with Cousin Alida, who was failing badly. When I came home again Mother told me that she had engaged Tony Morelli as a house man and that he had already moved into Dennis and Kate's old rooms over the carriage house.

I try to remember now whether I felt any special interest or premonition when she told me, any chill down my spine or even a particular awareness of Tony as a person, but I can't recall anything at all of the sort. I was relieved that we had someone to do the work because since Dennis had left it had piled up and Moses was very unsatisfactory and not always available when needed. Relieved. That was really all.

April 20th

10

It is more than two weeks since Grace was here. I might be able to put her out of my mind, as you put aside a disturbing dream, if it were not for Kent. "When is Auntie Grace coming again?" he has asked me nearly every day. "I know she's coming," he insists. "She'll want to see where my horse lives." He has not let me forget her, and when I think of her, all I can think of is her mad, insane demand that I hand Kent over to her.

I go to the post office every day, dreading to see a letter with a Philadelphia postmark, but so far there has been none. I try to tell myself that she has regretted her impulsive demand and sent the horse as a way of ending the affair gracefully, as a man will send a girl a five-pound box of candy to wind up a flirtation that no longer interests him—or so the girls at Miss Foote's used to say. But I can't quite believe it; the horse was too lavish a present for that, and besides there is too much determination in Grace's soft-looking chin to let her give up so soon. So I wait uneasily and wonder.

Why should she want *my* child? I wouldn't want hers.

It is not mine she wants, of course, it is Tony's. She obviously loved Tony. She was married to him—or thought she was—she lived with him for a year and a half and she still loved him. Was it the same Tony I knew, I wonder? Aren't we all different people to each new person we meet, or are there some who are so strongly, solidly themselves that they are the same to everyone? I feel that I am a chameleon myself, and probably Tony was too.

He did not meet *her* as a man out of work, eager for any job that would pay him enough to get something to eat and a place to sleep. (He slept that first night in Ewingville, he told me later, at Ellwood's and Ellwood not only did not charge him anything but lent him his razor in the morning. He got his supper at the quick lunch counter across the road from the station. A horrid place.) But when he met Grace he had the money Mother had entrusted to him; perhaps he had prospered in his business; he must have had an air of success about him. I wish I knew. At any rate he was gay, he was handsome, he had good manners.

And now she wants his child. I suppose she sees Tony in Kent, like Dido bearing young Ascanius in her bosom. Grandfather read the *Aeneid* to me in Dryden's translation. He loved it. I can remember how it moved him.

> *Or in her bosom young Ascanius bears,*
> *And seeks the father's image in the child*
> *If love by likeness might be so beguil'd.*

He used to read it and sigh and say, "That's very touching."

Odd. I've just thought of something. Aeneas like Tony was "a wand'ring guest, who from his country fled" and

Dido admitted "the dear perfidious man" to her "nuptial bed." But which of us is Dido, Grace or I? At any rate, it isn't seeing Tony in Kent—though certainly the child looks like his father—that endears Kent to me; it is much more seeing his great-grandfather's mind in him and the love that I feel he has for this old, not so very beautiful land that bred and nourished so many generations of Ewings. And of course something deeper and more biological, the invisible umbilical cord. He is mine as he never was Tony's.

But there is precedent in literature for Grace's feeling and no doubt in life too. The worst of it is that she has captured Kent's imagination. She won him at a single throw, with that preposterous toy.

"Mama, when is Auntie Grace coming?"

"Mama, Auntie Grace will be pleased to see how I can ride, won't she?"

"Mama, do you know who I think is the nicest person in the whole world?"

He has had no trouble at all in keeping the two Auntie Graces, the person and the horse, separate in his mind.

"I'm grooming Auntie Grace for the county fair. Can I have some red ribbons to plait in her tail?"

"I *can* plait too. Come see how I plaited Auntie Grace's tail."

He looks at me outraged when I give a hysterical squawk of laughter and sideswipes my chair with a kick as he goes out in dudgeon to commune with Auntie Grace—both of them, I suppose.

Auntie Grace. Auntie Grace. Auntie Grace. All day long. Over and over again.

"That's enough about Auntie Grace," I snapped this afternoon, goaded beyond endurance. "If you say Auntie Grace once more today I'll spank you."

His face darkened and his eyes flashed. "Auntie Grace! Auntie Grace! Auntie Grace!" he shouted.

So of course I had to spank him. He'd have had the upper hand of me entirely if I hadn't. I turned him over my knee so fast he hadn't time to struggle and gave him six sharp slaps with the palm of my hand. He tautened his muscles and made his little backside so hard that it was like hitting a board with your bare hand. I realized for the first time that the old cliché, "This hurts me more than it hurts you," which I had always taken for pious claptrap, was literally true.

He yelled as though I were killing him, and I laughed as I let him up. "We're a fine pair," I said, and flicked his nose lightly with my forefinger, an affectionate gesture which I used rather rarely. But he was not to be mollified. He went off scowling and has been very remote and unsmiling ever since, but so far he has not uttered the forbidden name again.

He is in bed and asleep now. The evening is warm and the window is open on the garden. From the damp places in the wood behind the house the spring peepers are shrilling. What sort of a mother am I? How is this child to be brought up without a father? What would Tony have done with him? I am seized with sudden, sharp, suffocating pain of a kind that I thought I had put behind me forever. If only Tony had come back to me, successful and confident as he went to her, if only he had lived, if only we were a family of three, not two.

April 22nd

11

Kent has changed the name of his horse to Dusty. He has not told me so, but the words "Auntie Grace" are no longer heard in the land and he informs me casually that Dusty has been a little off her oats but is feeling better now.

I took him to the ice-cream parlor and treated him to a double portion of ice cream, one for him and one for Dusty. We are on excellent terms, my son and I.

April 23rd

12

It was Mother who first told me Tony's history, not Tony himself.

"He comes of a very good family, actually," she reported. "His father was a priest who rebelled against the Church and left it."

I could see that it was to his credit in Mother's Protestant eyes that the father had seen the light and broken his vows. To Mother, too, an Italian priest had the same social standing as an Episcopal rector in America. I wondered but I said nothing. Mother and I were on each other's nerves at that time and I kept any differences of opinion to myself as far as I could.

"His mother was a Protestant, an English girl living in Italy. She was a governess, it seems, in a wealthy Italian family. Her parents were dead but they were professional people and she had had a good education. So they were married and Tony was born. But the little town would not accept them—a former priest, married and excommunicated—and they had a desperate struggle and finally died of consumption, both of them. It is a sad little story. Tony went to England to try to find his mother's people. He got some help from a cousin, a middle-aged woman, and came to this country."

For myself, I did not believe it. I never have. The story was too perfectly tailored to disarm Mother and to appeal to her romantic imagination. Besides, Tony was too good with his hands. They were lean, sinewy hands with spatulate finger tips and he could do anything with them, transplant seedlings, clip a hedge, mend a spigot, wax a floor, beat a carpet, refinish furniture, carve a knob to take the place of one that was lost. I did not think he had been a farmer or a day laborer, but I was sure he had worked with his hands in some way, as a carpenter, perhaps, or a handyman, or a craftsman of some sort.

His English was good. He mixed up his v's and w's and he lengthened his short i's into ee's, but he made few grammatical mistakes, though he was sometimes at a loss for a word. His a's were broader than ours in South Jersey. He might well have got his English from an English mother, and not a Cockney either.

As the fall darkened into winter and there was less work to do out of doors, before the snows came, he had more time to himself and he used it to do over the furniture in his rooms. The small bedroom and sitting room over the carriage house were furnished with castoffs from the attic which had suffered a good deal from neglect and from green paint, to which Dennis's predecessor had been addicted. He mended the legs of a slat-backed chair, patiently sandpapered the paint off and rubbed the old cherry wood with linseed oil; from somewhere he got rushes and re-rushed the seat. It was only an old battered Ware chair from Salem, but when he had finished with it it looked like new. A chest of drawers with a bulging front took longer. He kept that in the harness room for weeks, working at it whenever he had spare time. I used to stop and watch him at work and talk with him. I had an idea, the more fool I, that as long as I did not sit down with him I was keeping the social distance inviolate between us.

"Thees one is made of walnut," I remember his saying in that slow, soft voice of his, "and there is a fine little line of lighter wood set into it—see?"

"Oh, yes. Inlay we call it. Clever of you to see it, buried under all that dirt."

He ran his hand lovingly over the wood where he had cleaned it. "It is fine wood. Feel how smooth."

Once we got on the subject of hands.

"I read palms," he said.

"You mean you tell fortunes?"

"No, not exactly. But I look at a palm and see what that person is like and what his destiny will be. You don't believe me?"

I shook my head. "It sounds like pure superstition to me."

"Take my hand, for instance," he said, extending it palm upward. "That's my life line. It breaks off suddenly here. That might mean—it usually would mean, in fact— an early death, but look at my line of fortune; see how it is very long and strong. So that makes up for the break in my life line. And look at the Mount of Mercury, here, how well developed that is. That means I am a man of much industry with an aptitude for commerce."

Almost without thinking I turned my own palm up and looked at it, seeing the deeply incised pale chain-like lines, the pink mounds, the faint bluish veins as if for the first time. He took it in his own, squeezing it a little to deepen the lines, turning it toward the light. His touch was warm and light and strong; a thrill went up my arm as if there were something electric about it.

"Now *you* have a very long, strong life line. You will live to a great old age. And," he added, "you will be a beautiful old lady."

"How nice," I said sarcastically. "Only forty or fifty years to wait."

"You do not believe me, but it is true. You will see. You will have a profile like a cameo and all that bushy dull-red hair will be white and very lovely. You will look commanding."

I felt myself flushing and I knew that a blush was not becoming to me; my neck got mottled and my face turned a dark, brick-like red. He gave me an odd side-long look from under his thick black lashes as he bent his head again over my hand.

"What a head line!" he exclaimed. "How strong and clear! But your heart line is pale and weak. Such a peety. Wait. Let me see your other hand."

It was all lies and make-believe, or it was a form of flirtation, or both. I was not deceived but I was, in spite of myself, interested and somehow charmed. I gave him my left hand to inspect, that is to say, to grasp in his, to turn and squeeze, to tip this way and that. By this time we were both sitting on the old broken-down sofa that he had brought to the harness room to work on at some future time.

"The left hand shows what nature gave you, the right shows what you have made of it. See, it is as I thought. Your heart line by nature is delicate and deep, but your right hand shows you have let it go to nothing, almost."

He spoke severely. I thought he was making fun of me—as no doubt he was. I snatched my hand away and stood up. "This is very foolish talk," I said, "and I am interrupting your work."

64

"*Si, signorina,*" he murmured, and there was a mocking tone in his voice.

I retreated and presently I heard him singing. He used to sing a good deal as he went about his work. He had a lovely voice.

Later I learned that he got all his knowledge of palmistry from a little black book with a silver hand on the cover. It was the only book I ever saw Tony read. Unconsciously I despised him for not being a reader, which was ill done of me. Grace would not have made the same mistake. No doubt her heart line is rich and fruity. Her head line is pretty good too, I imagine. As for despising, Tony might well have despised me for my total lack of musical knowledge. I did not even know that it was arias from operas he was singing, though in time I came to recognize "La donna e mobile."

We had more and more frequent little talks together snatched out of the day: when he brought in wood for the stoves, when he was splitting logs in the stable yard, when he polished the brass or the silver. Sometimes we talked about his impressions of America and how it differed from Europe. He was critical about America, repeating all the old charges of dollar-worshiping and railing at the ugliness of the churches, and I would answer him hotly; then I would catch the gleam in his eye and realize that he had been talking that way at least partly to tease me. Sometimes I told him my impressions of Italy. We were in Venice, Florence, Assisi and Rome, a few days each, that first trip abroad. I came to know that sidelong glance of Tony's well, but he did not touch my hands again.

How much did Mother notice? I wonder. Was she aware at all of how often I made excuses to be where Tony was, or how much time he spent with a tool or a cloth idle in his hands while he held forth entertainingly on some subject far removed from Ewingville? But Mother too was listening to Tony, listening and talking. She was giving him advice, teaching him ways and manners of our country, instructing him in the history of South Jersey and its old families. In return he flattered her openly. She was *bellissima* and *simpatica*, the most kind lady.

He was young and full of urgent life, handsome, naïf, eager to learn and to get ahead. He was saving his money, he told us, to go into business some day for himself, but he was in no hurry, for he was happy in Ewingville with us.

And Ewingville, which had been so dull—Lord, how dull it was, after our last trip abroad!—Ewingville was much less dull with Tony about the house.

April 24th

13

I missed Father greatly after he died, and I reproached myself because I had not appreciated him more while he was living. He had always been there in the background, never asserting himself very much, well liked by the other men in Ewingville and the county seat, going to his office and coming back at regular hours, worrying us, or perhaps annoying was the word, by insisting on keeping Black Jack and driving him.

Father adored Mother. That was the foundation stone on which our life was built. He worshiped the ground she walked on. There is one who kisses and one who turns the cheek. Mother turned the cheek. She was ten years younger than he was. Now that I am grown up— thirty-seven, the same age Mother was when Father was killed—I don't think ten years such a very great matter, but Mother did. The way she dramatized herself, to the very end, she was the cherished flower-like young wife of an old man, and I took her version of it at face value.

Father accepted it too. Whatever Mother thought was right for him.

Father was stout. He wore pince-nez over his small, bright, quick, marble-like brown eyes. He liked good food. He knew food, as a connoisseur knows paintings or sculpture, only more so, of course, for he absorbed it literally, not figuratively, and he was fussy about it. He was really upset and out of temper if something went wrong and good material was spoiled in the cooking, if it was underdone or overdone or badly seasoned or if a sauce curdled. We kept guinea fowl in those days—hateful, noisy creatures always squawking "Come back! Come back!"—because Father was fond of breast of guinea hen on thin slices of Virginia ham. We had asparagus in the garden, which was cut just before it was cooked and always served with Hollandaise sauce, the real, not the mock, and it *would* curdle sometimes, which was a black tragedy. We watched eagerly for the first shad running in the Delaware in the spring, and we had planked shad with wedges of lemon and rosettes of mashed potatoes around the edges of the plank and the great fish in the center, flaky and rich and browned to perfection. In the fall he would get a barrel of oysters from Bivalve and they would be kept in the cellar and fed corn meal, so that we could have oysters on the half shell at any moment we—Father, that is—desired. He liked sweet things too, angel food, high and white and airy, and peach ice cream made on the back porch with peaches from our own tree and thick yellow cream from the farm, lemon meringue pie with the meringue tender and delicately brown. Once the meringue was tough and came off the pie all in a piece and you might have thought that Kate had tried to poison him from the way he took on. He liked to go out shooting railbirds in the marshes in the fall, and we had them, small, brown and glazed, riding on rafts of toast. We had frogs' legs and terrapin and soft-shelled crabs in season, and creamed sweetbreads as other people have ham and eggs.

I find I enjoy remembering the food we used to have and take a certain pride in Father's gourmet knowledge —from a safe distance. I used to think it was all a great fuss about nothing very much and to enjoy what Father termed the uneatable grub at Cousin Alida's. "Fried chicken is all that Southern darky of hers can rise to," he would say with a chuckle, "and those overrated beaten biscuits that are no better than ordinary Trenton crackers."

Mother took pleasure in setting a good table, though it was a strain, too, and after Father's death she relaxed. And so did whoever was in the kitchen.

While Father was alive he and Mother entertained a good bit, mostly his business friends and their wives. They were always enthusiastic about the food and there was a lot of joking about Father's waistline, which he took in good part. There was a bustle in the house all day when there was to be a party in the evening, and afterwards if it had gone well and the cooking had been up to standard I could hear Mother and Father talking it over late in bed, their voices low but satisfied, with an occasional burst of laughter erupting into the hollow silence of the house.

When nobody was coming in Father liked to read in the evenings, sitting in his stationary rocker (which he sat through, three times) in the library on one side of the big oblong center table. Mother sat on the other side, sharing the light of the large bronze lamp, reading too. I was supposed to be doing my homework at the desk, with a small lamp of my own, but usually I was reading too—at that time mostly the insipid novels of Rosa Nouchette Carey or Charlotte Yonge.

Father liked to kick off his shoes with one foot against the heel of the other and sit in his stocking feet, a habit which Mother considered infra dig, on a level with sitting in one's shirt sleeves and suspenders or eating in the kitchen. She tried to persuade him to put on slippers when he came home and even trained me in the pretty filial gesture, culled from English novels, of bringing Father his slippers in the library, but it was no use. He liked to kick off his shoes; he did not like, he said, to have his daughter waiting on him as if he were in his dotage.

Father's office was on east Main Street, the same one that Ned Wadsworth has now. He had the insurance agency, sold real estate—but not much of it, in Ewingville—did conveyancing, drew up wills, gave legal advice about every sort of civil dispute; he never handled criminal cases. He was kind and sensible and people trusted him. We never knew till afterwards, Mother and I, how many persons he helped without charging them anything at all. The church was jammed at his funeral with a lot of people we had never seen before, people who lived in the side streets of Exeter, farmers from the country round, and, of course, all of Ewingville. Many of them came to see Mother afterwards, to tell her how much they owed him. In their halting and often ungrammatical phrases they built up a picture of him that was strange to us, of a genial, open, hail-fellow-well-met, simple man who could tell uproariously funny stories—not the kind, excuse me, ma'am, he would tell before a lady.

In the summers Father sent Mother and me off to the White Mountains for a month, where we stayed in a large frame hotel with long porches and rows on rows of rocking chairs. Mother spent all spring getting a wardrobe together for changing her clothes three times a day.

She had friends there whom she met year after year and with whom she made up an envied inner clique that lorded it over the transients and newcomers and social climbers who never made the grade. They arranged coaching trips to the notches and such like excursions, inviting an occasional favored outsider to join them and incidentally to contribute her share of the cost. As for me, I was in heaven, with a crowd of girls and boys of my own age with whom to climb mountains, play croquet and "go swimming," which meant mostly splashing about and shrieking, in the pool formed by damming up the icy mountain brook behind the hotel. Father stayed home in the role of indulgent and hard-worked husband and father, but he enjoyed having the house to himself for a while, I am sure. When he got tired of that he went off to Manasquan with some of what Mother called his cronies for surf fishing.

Father was born on a farm down Salem way, not one of the old prosperous farms but a tract of ill-lying, infertile land with a gaunt graceless house rearing up out of a welter of barnyard fences and derelict farm machinery and a tilted privy prominently displayed. His parents, Willie and May Dobson, were hard workers but fatally unlucky. Nothing ever went right. The flock of turkeys which they were counting on for cash money got their feet wet and died. It always rained before the hay was in. The creek flooded and the wheat rotted on the stalk. Their cows contracted hoof and mouth disease when no other cattle for miles around got it.

Father, who had to do chores early and late, vowed as a small boy he would never be a farmer. He went through the district school, walking two miles each way to get there and milking the young teacher of every drop of knowledge that he possessed. After that he ran away to Exeter, got a job sweeping floors and emptying spittoons in the courthouse and enrolled in the high school. Grandfather's eye fell on him, and from then on he had a friend and guide and backer. He was not the only ambitious country boy whom Grandfather launched, but he was the one who stayed closest to the Judge. After working his way through college—Rutgers, it was—he came back to the county seat and read law in Grandfather's office. He was often at our house, to get a square meal, Grandfather said, and to do odd jobs of correspondence and other business for Grandfather. When Father was ready for it, Grandfather eased him into the office on Main Street and he was on his way.

Cousin Alida told me that Father got Mother on the rebound. It was soon after Father's death, and I had come to see Cousin Alida to tell her that I was leaving school because Mother needed me at home and to get the overnight things and other clothes that I kept at her house for when I stayed over with her in bad weather.

I always loved the room that was called mine at Cousin Alida's. It was the third story back, with a sunny bay window facing south and overlooking the back yard, which had a high wooden fence painted brown and an ailanthus tree and iron lace garden furniture on a little plot of rather sooty grass. My room had a walnut bed with a carved headboard that mounted to the ceiling, a bureau of curly maple and a chiffonier to match, a pier glass and a great carved walnut wardrobe whose doors creaked.

Cousin Alida came into the room as I was drearily stowing away my things into my grip and sat on the window seat, which was upholstered in pink-flowered cretonne to match the curtains. She was older than Mother but just as pretty in her own way, which was of the petite, French-marquise order: fluffy white hair that might have been powdered, exquisitely chiseled features in a little pointed face, an elegant pincushion of a figure

72

and tiny hands and feet. A widow of many years standing, she had shocked me to the marrow when I was twelve by saying what I have since heard so often that I recognize it for the crude bit of folklore that it is but which I then thought newly minted by my cynical cousin: "A widow is the best thing to be, Roberta. If you're married your husband bosses you and if you're single everyone despises you." "Father *never* bosses Mother!" I cried indignantly. To which she replied cryptically, "Ah, that's worse still." And now I am a widow myself.

That day, as I was packing, she settled herself on the window seat, her feet not quite reaching the floor, and began without preliminary:

"It's perfect nonsense, you know, your giving up school—and in the middle of the term too. Your mother doesn't need you any more than a dog needs side pockets, and even if she did you need an education more."

"You don't understand Mother," I said.

"Yes, I do—more than you think. But that's beside the point. You ought to finish school and go to college."

"College?"

"Don't shriek at me, Roberta. It's rude. College."

College for girls is commonplace enough now, but it was an extraordinary idea then. I had read, it is true, two books about college girls, *The Three Vassar Girls on the Rhine* and *The Three Vassar Girls on the Nile*, and had been temporarily attracted toward college, until I had realized that it was perfectly possible to go direct to those interesting rivers without going round by Vassar College first.

"What is there for you at Ewingville?" pursued Cousin Alida relentlessly. "You've got a good brain. What are you going to do with it down there in the pine barrens?"

"We *don't* live in the pine barrens!"

"Go to college and get out into the world. Besides, suppose you ever had to support yourself, what could you do? You couldn't teach even small children without having finished school. All you could do would be to sell ribbons in a store."

"I shan't ever have to support myself. Father has made good provision for Mother and me."

It was then that she told me what I still think she should have kept to herself.

"Your mother is making a great play over being prostrated with grief by her great loss, but actually she took your father on the rebound. She was head over heels in love with Tench Tilghman, who was in the First City Troop with my husband. He paid her some attention when she visited us—no more than any young man pays any very pretty visiting girl—and she took it seriously. Then when he married Christine Alexander, as everyone knew he would, what did your mother do but bounce off and marry your father's clerk! Don't go and make a mess of your life before it's even begun out of mistaken filial devotion."

It made no difference of course. But those were barbed words and they clung to my mind like beggar needles to a wool skirt.

I see I have written two things about Father that might seem contradictory. I have said that he could never compete with Mother and that I missed him greatly after he died. Both are true. It was Mother who filled my mind, Mother with whom I did things, Mother who made the decisions about me. But it was Father I went to when I was hurt or disappointed or felt more than usually inadequate. He never said very much but he listened; he made me know, somehow, that he loved me as I was and had faith in me. He was *there*, and while he was there I was safe.

Besides, a house dies when the man goes out of it. It breathes through him. It breathes in when he is being taken his shaving water and his newly polished shoes and eating his breakfast; lets the breath out when he goes off to the office and everything is suddenly quiet; breathes in again when he comes home for lunch, and out when the women take their naps; takes a big breath when dinner is in the making and the women are dressing and finally he comes home, tired and dispirited or successful and elated, full of the events of the day; breathes out slowly and luxuriously as he settles down content after dinner to the long leisurely evening. The clocks—the grandfather clock in the parlor, the Seth Thomas in the library, the busy little French gilt clock with its nervous chimes in the sitting room, the bronze monstrosity in the dining room and the plain wooden wall clock with the loud tick in the kitchen—all wait for him to wind them. The people in the kitchen, no matter how much lip service they pay to the mistress, really put themselves out to please the master. He is the one who counts with them. And they are right.

I am Father's daughter as much as Mother's, the granddaughter of Willie and May Dobson—though I seldom saw them—as much as of Sarah Ellis and Judge Ewing. What did Father have to give me? Or, perhaps more to the point, what if anything did I take from him? His kindness? His bonhomie? (Certainly not that.) His love of good food? His—was it patience or humility or acceptance? His worship of Mother? His dogged refusal to be pushed any more than just so far? There must be something else, something I am not seeing. I cannot find anything of Father in me. I must be, as Mother used to say I was, all Ewing.

April 25th

14

She has been here again. She came without warning. Kent went to the door, for I was up in the attic putting away woolens with a cloth tied over my head, and the first thing I knew about it was a joyous shriek from him:

"Mama! Mama! Auntie Grace is here and we're going on a picnic!"

Snatching off my headcloth and dropping my apron on the newel post, I hurried downstairs looking no doubt like a witch. At any rate I felt like one.

There she was, packed into a black tailor-made suit with a white shirtwaist and a stiff black straw hat with shiny black chicken-feather wings riding high on her yellow pompadour, standing in the hall inside the door, while Ellwood sat grinning in his hack in the driveway outside. On the seat beside him was a covered basket.

"Oh," was all I could manage to say.

"Now I'm not going to make you any trouble at all. I just came on impulse and there wasn't any time to write you. Yesterday was such a beautiful day I thought why don't I go down to Ewingville tomorrow and take that dear little boy for an outing, so I had my cook fry some chicken and so on and pack a lunch—and here I am!"

Kent was dancing around me in a state of high excitement, jumping up and down and clutching at my sleeve to secure my attention.

"Ellwood's going to drive us out to the river, Mama, and we're going to have a picnic there. Mama, we're going to have a picnic on the river!"

I looked at her accusingly. "This is not fair," I said. "You ought not to have done it."

"Oh, but you must come too, of course. I counted on that. I thought that, while Kent played around, you and I could have a quiet talk."

I was flustered and confused and divided. It was outrageous of her to come here like this, outrageous and highhanded and arrogant. She had smoothly taken advantage of me a second time, for with Kent in ecstasy how could I send her away? And yet, angry as I was, I felt a subcurrent of longing, like the tide pulling the sand away from around your feet, to have that quiet talk, to find out where she had met Tony, how it had all happened. But I was damned—yes, damned is the word; "Swear me a good, mouth-filling oath, Kate"—if I was going to go out at her bidding and eat her food.

At that moment my guardian angel—occasionally I like to pretend that I have one—bestirred himself. Clouds had been gathering as we talked, and now they opened and let down the last shower of April on us. Rain pattered and then it drummed; wind drove it against the windows and across the threshold into the hall.

"You can't possibly go out in this," I said. "You'll have to stay here." I nodded dismissal to Ellwood. "We shan't need you any longer," I called to him.

"Wait a minute! Ellwood, bring in that basket, please,

and come back in time for me to get the two fifty-seven. The two fifty-seven, not the five o'clock. Have you got that straight?"

Kent's big brown eyes were swimming in tears. "It'll clear up," he pleaded. "It's sure to clear up."

She knelt before him and put her arms around him while Ellwood set the basket on the table behind her. "Never mind, darling, we'll have the picnic right here. That will be fun too, won't it?"

"Fried chicken and chocolate cake, like you said?"

"Yes, all of it, just the same. We can sit on the floor, too, if you like."

"I'll get lunch for us," I said firmly. "No guest in my house will ever bring her own food."

She stood up smiling. "But an uninvited guest—"

"We have simple fare but plenty of it, and anyone who comes is welcome to share it."

So I took her again to the antiquated bathroom, showed her into the spare room to lay off her hat and jacket, and left Kent to entertain her while I prepared lunch. I steadied myself by concentrating with all my might on what I was doing.

I set the table with Irish damask and an Irish crochet centerpiece, on which I put a silver bowl of apple blossoms. I used the old plain silver, made by Richardson in Philadelphia before 1800, which I like better than the fancy stuff from Baltimore that Mother had in her trousseau, and the Lowestoft china instead of the everyday Canton. As a last touch I got down the precious old Ewing glass goblets from the china closet and took the time to wash them with ammonia and polish them with a chamois skin. They shone like diamonds and rang musically when I snapped my finger against them.

All the style of the meal had to be in the appointments, for what I had planned for Kent and me was country sausage from the farm with cream gravy and hot cakes and I wasn't going to change it for her. I did add home-made pickles and we had my spiced peaches for dessert, with angel food. As a treat I made coffee and my coffee is good. I don't usually have it for lunch.

By the time that I was ready—and considerably calmed down—the shower was over and I had to call them in from the stable where Kent was displaying Dusty's (thank heaven he changed its name!) living arrangements to his Auntie Grace.

Grace exclaimed over the glass and china.

"This is Lowestoft, I know, and is this Wistar glass?"

"No, it's Ewing glass."

"Oh. They have some Wistar glass at Bailey's and it's very expensive." She lost interest in my glass and turned her attention to the food, which she said was delicious, though really she just picked at it. But I imagine the situation was embarrassing enough to spoil her appetite anyhow. Kent had a red and white fringed napkin spread out on the floor, where he stuffed himself with fried chicken, deviled eggs, jelly sandwiches and chocolate layer cake from Grace's basket. After lunch she brought a jigsaw puzzle out of the basket for him.

"It's very inexpensive," she said apologetically to me. "I understand how you feel about presents, but I just couldn't come to see a child without bringing him something and I thought this would occupy him while we talk."

But before we could settle down to that talk she took some photographs out of her handbag to show us.

"This is my nephew Johnny. He's seven now. That was taken in the snow last year with his new sled. And this is Helen, who's five—just your age, Kent. And this is Ralph; he's the youngest. He's four. There's Johnny again on his pony. And here he is with his tricycle.

That's Helen in her bathing suit. Isn't she cute? And here they all are on the beach at Spring Lake."

As Kent pored over them, fascinated, she handed me a little water-color sketch of a house to look at. It was a towering frame erection made of scalloped shingles painted white, garlanded with two tiers of piazzas, with an impressive branching staircase leading up to the lower tier, and two towers, one on each of the front corners. The tower on the right was round, with a flat top edged with a railing, and the one on the left was square, topped with a tall steeple shingled in Kelly green to match the mansard roof. I took a secret malicious pleasure in the sheer bad taste and ugliness of it.

"That's the family cottage at Spring Lake," she said complacently. "We all go there in the summer, my parents and my sister and her children and I. As you can see, there's plenty of room for everybody. The beach is right in front. Look, darling, this is where Auntie Grace goes in the summer. See those windows in the tower? That's where I used to sleep when I was a little girl. I could see the ocean and sometimes a school of porpoises all jumping and diving and sometimes boats and always sea gulls."

But the "cottage" was less interesting to Kent than the children. Johnny he appeared to regard with a touch of awe, but Helen, who was just his age, must have seemed to him more accessible. He wanted to know all about her. Did she have a rocking horse? Did she go bathing in the ocean? Was it Helen who made that castle in the sand? Grace gave him the photographs to hold in his own hands and then to spread out on the floor and pore over.

"You'll have to come to Spring Lake some time and play with Johnny and Helen and Ralph on the beach. Maybe your mama will bring you."

"When?" He turned to her a face so blazing with delight that she felt obliged to dampen the fires hastily. "Oh, not now. In the summer some time, maybe."

She had one last photograph, of her parents, who live in Germantown. Her father is a manufacturer of textiles.

"Let me see," said Kent, inserting his curly head between my hands, but finding nothing noteworthy in the well-dressed, prosperous-looking elderly pair, he returned to the children on the floor. Grace said to me in a low voice, "I want to tell you first of all that I've decided to take back my first husband's name. That won't surprise anybody, because I was married so much longer to Mr. Peacock and it was his house and his money and all. Besides," she added realistically, "of course it's a better name than Morelli."

"You were married before?" I had thought that Peacock was her maiden name.

"Yes, didn't I tell you? I was married for nine years. We had one child, a little boy, but we lost him. Mr. Peacock passed away three years ago, of a heart attack."

"I'm sorry," I murmured. "You have had a great deal of trouble."

"Yes, I have. But this last is the worst, somehow. A trouble you can't talk about seems to eat inward, like, if you know what I mean. I haven't told anybody about Anthony being married to you, not even my parents, except Father Doyle—he's our priest. He was so shocked and grieved, poor man."

"Yes, I should think he might be."

"Our little boy, Roland, passed away in his second summer, of summer complaint. The doctor did everything—he stayed all night and worked over him—but it was no use. He would have been ten now. My sister has three and I want a child of my own so dreadfully. You

81

can see why I want Kent so much and how I'd love him and do for him—"

I stopped her with a gesture of my hand. "Little pitchers," I warned.

"He's not listening. I'd tell people he was the son of Anthony's cousin, and he could go right on calling me Auntie Grace. Unless, of course, he himself wanted to say Mother. I wish you would go and talk to Father Doyle. I'll give you a note to him. He could tell you all about me and satisfy you. And I'll give you Mr. Kirkpatrick's—that's my lawyer—name and address too."

"Please. I am really not in the least interested in your proposition. What can I say to convince you?"

"You ought to know all the facts before you dismiss it out of hand. Either Penn Charter or Episcopal Academy, you know, and summers at Spring Lake with the other children. He needs other children desperately. You must see that yourself. All right, I won't say any more now, but you owe it to him to at least look at it from all sides."

The question that has been swelling inside of me these last three weeks and more burst out of me then.

"Where did you first meet Tony?"

"Through Father Doyle. That's one reason why he feels so terrible about it now. But he had no idea, of course. He told me that a young man who'd been very unfortunate had come to him needing work and asked me if I had any furniture that wanted mending."

"Needing work?"

"Yes. He had been very unfortunate. His partner had cheated him out of all his savings and he was nearly desperate."

"What was his partner's name?"

"His name was Alf Brown. Did you know him? They'd had a little business in New York—manufacturing buttons, I think it was—and the partner swindled Anthony completely and absconded with all his money."

All Mother's money. So that was what happened. And all this time I have been imagining Tony going to Grace successful and confident.

"So I gave him an old table that I was going to get rid of to fix up and he worked in the stable."

"And then you offered him a room over the stable."

"Yes. I gave up the horses after Mr. Peacock passed away, and the coachman's room was empty. How did you know?"

"I guessed."

"He was really very expert. You know people are going crazy about what they call antiques now, fixing up all sorts of stuff out of attics and second-hand stores, and Tony soon had all the work he could do. We went into partnership and set up a shop in the stable. We were talking about moving it to Spring Garden Street and adding a decorating department when—when—"

"How long did it take him?" I interrupted her—brutally, as I look back on it. I am ashamed of myself.

"I don't know what you mean. How long did what take him?"

"To marry you."

She flushed. "You needn't put it like that," she said with some dignity. "He came in the spring and we were married during Christmas week." Her eyes filled up as they had the first day she came, and she dabbed at them with her black-bordered handkerchief.

In a surge of real feeling for her I put my hand on her knee. "Don't cry. He wasn't worth crying over. Tony was a rascal, really, you know." I meant it literally, not in the joking way you tell a child he's a rascal.

"Yes, I used to say to him sometimes, You rascal! But he wasn't, to me. Oh, I know now that he sinned, terribly. But I didn't know it then. We were very happy. I miss him as I knew him then. Perhaps there's something wrong with me, but it doesn't seem to matter very much what he was before I knew him. I am very sorry for you, I truly am. But I think you have to take people as you know them yourself, don't you—not as somebody else knew them?"

"Perhaps," I agreed reluctantly. I was remembering a story I read in an old book I found on Charing Cross Road in London, *Tales and Legends of the Scottish Highlands* or some such thing. "There was an old story about a Highland girl who met a handsome young man and fell in love with him and married him. When he was out one day she found out—I forget how—that he was a water kelpie and she was horrified. She ran home to her parents and never saw him again. I always thought it was poor-spirited of her. They had been happy together; she'd only known him as a handsome young man."

"What's a water kelpie?"

"It's a horse that lives in lakes and rivers and takes human form sometimes."

"But that's different. That's not human. I think she was right."

A loud thumping on the front door made us both jump.

"Mercy! That must be Ellwood."

She was gone in a flurry, taking the basket with her but forgetting the photographs. She manages always to plant something in Kent that will grow. Perhaps she did not intend to leave the photographs behind—though certainly the name and address of her lawyer written on the back of her calling card and propped against the amethyst glass bottle on my bureau was no accident—but Kent has played with them all evening as a little girl plays with paper dolls. Johnny, Helen and Ralph have supplanted Dusty, née Auntie Grace, in his heart and mind.

What a day.

April 30

15

Tony left me on June 15th, 1891. I did not know that it was to be an end; I thought of it as the promise of a new beginning. He was going to join his friend Alf Brown—such a dreadful name—and they were going to start a button factory. Tony was to design the buttons—he had made me a lovely set like tiny wild roses carved out of wood—and supply the capital; Mr. Brown had the business knowledge and the connections, and he had written that he had found the ideal property in New York which they would use if they could buy it right away.

The capital of course was supplied by Mother. I think I have written that most of Mother's money went with Tony. How difficult it is to be completely truthful. Most of it went when Father died and stopped making money. When his will was probated and his affairs settled, it had turned out that there wasn't as much as Mother thought there would be. He had expected to live much longer, of course, and he had spent his money freely; our way of living was not inexpensive. He did not leave much more than his life insurance, and Mother dipped into that for our trips abroad and for what turned out to be an unfortunate speculation in western land. We had the house and the farm, which Mother had inherited from her father, and her annuity; but there was little left by 1891, and Mother decided to entrust most of it to Tony for this venture, which she hoped would restore what had been frittered away.

The decision had not been reached lightly or quickly. For months they had talked about it. They had long, serious, intimate discussions from which I was excluded, partly because I had the baby to take care of and partly because I was not entirely in sympathy with the project. The fact is, I was in conflict with myself about it. Mother believed Tony's story about his origins; I did not. I would have liked to see Alf Brown for myself. I would have hung back, have given Tony part of the money he wanted but not all of it at once. On the other hand I never came out and spoke strongly against it because I wanted so much to believe in it. With all my heart I wanted Tony to be successful, not to get rich but just to make enough so that he could send for me to join him with the baby and we could have a little home of our own and a life of our own away from Ewingville. So, half distrusting, half hoping, I was not enthusiastically with them; I was dragging my heels and they both felt it. It dimmed their joy, detracted from their confidence. And by holding back I threw them even closer together.

Was I jealous of Mother in regard to Tony? I suppose I was. They got along so well. Mother liked Tony from the first. She believed in him. She treated him indulgently and admiringly and as if they two had a special understanding, the kind of understanding that could only be possible between two people who were beautiful physically and had the particular inborn certainty of superiority that seems to go with the possession of that kind of beauty. I know that Mother felt it about herself; she always carried her own beauty as if it were a moral as well as a physical endowment and as if it gave her a manifest superiority over the common run of people. She recognized it too in others and yielded them the sort of acknowledgment and respect that a brave knight in the days of chivalry yielded another knight. It was a bond—and also a contest of strength, like jousting—between her and Cousin Alida. It was one reason why Mother, though she loved me because I was hers, pitied me. Scorned me, I almost wrote, but I think that may be an exaggeration. It was the reason why Tony's good looks opened the door for him into Mother's confidence. In that respect they met as equals, or at least as members of the same secret society or chivalric order: people who saw life with different eyes from the rest of humanity. I have wondered sometimes if the very rich don't meet each other on somewhat the same terms and with the same sort of mental outlook.

In any case, Mother and Tony started with this initial bond—or Mother did; Tony just made the most of whatever came his way. In addition there was the bond between the older person who gives and guides, generously and wisely, and the younger person who receives gratefully and gracefully.

And I? I was the pitiable and ludicrous homely old maid who—in Mother's eyes—had allowed my physical impulses to betray me, and who in Tony's eyes, I have sometimes thought, trapped him into marriage. Tony did not love me except, possibly, for a little while; I did not deceive myself about that. But he was pleased to have a son. He used to play with Kent, or Anthony Junior as he was then, a great deal and there was real tenderness and depth of feeling in his face when he looked down at the sleeping baby or held his little hands as he took his first lurching steps.

Tony flattered Mother openly and joyously. He never flattered me, but he had a way of telling me the truth about myself that was somehow better than flattery, as if he were taking the trouble to see the real me, as most people don't; they simply see in others the idea they themselves have got of them; as if he saw the real me and was still, in spite of the obvious lacks, a little amused by it and on the whole content with it. "You have no ear for music. Musically you are as ignorant as a savage in the jungle—more so. Listen! What is this? Ah, Roberta!" Or he would say, "You are too old to have such young feelings. Your feelings are as fresh and easily torn as a child's." More than once he told me that I would improve with age. "You make me think of a persimmon; it does not get its flavor till after the frost has come." I used to think that if we could only have a home of our own, just Tony and Kent and I, however simple it was, and if Tony had work that occupied him, we could make some sort of a life. So though I had not much faith in the New York venture, it was still the only hope I could see. Living at home with Tony in Mother's house was misery.

That day he left, the peonies were past but the roses were out everywhere. All of Ewingville was fragrant with them. The play of sunshine on our old stone house and of shade on the whitewashed fence, the fountain of silver moon roses over the front windows: I'll never forget how it looked. And the lawn brilliantly green, the air warm in the sun, cool in the shadows, and sweet, sweet, sweet.

He was taking the eleven o'clock train up. We are lucky to have such good train service, two in the morning, two in the afternoon, each way. Ellwood came for him, to take all his things, his wheel strapped on behind, the two grips which had been Father's, with his clothes and his designs and carvings. He even took the buttons he had made for me; I had to cut them off my plaid waist. He had come, two and a half years earlier, with nothing; he was leaving with two big grips full of clothes, a Columbia bicycle that had cost one hundred and twenty-five dollars and in the breast pocket of his new spring suit a wallet containing Mother's bonds.

Mother had planned that we were to say good-by to Tony on the front steps and stand there waving him off, me with the baby in my arms, but at the last minute I decided to ride to the station with him. I thrust the baby at her and climbed determinedly into the hack beside Tony. Ellwood touched his old mare with the whip and with a jerk we moved off, while Kent screamed and Mother exclaimed, "*Roberta!*"

"Now you look like a witch again," said Tony, "like you did the first day I saw you, only your face is clean."

I laughed. Somehow I never minded Tony's calling me a witch. For one thing he only did it when he was in high spirits, and that morning he was on top of his world. He wore a stiff straw hat, very slightly tilted on one side, and he had a rosebud in the buttonhole of his light gray suit. His dark eyes glowed, his profile was like a profile on a coin. All the village seemed to know that he was leaving to make his fortune in New York. People waved to him, and he responded by taking off his hat and waving it widely to them. A few called, "Good luck!" The village was more cordial to him as he left than it had ever been while he was here; he was a foreigner and as such, suspect; then there had been the scandal of our marriage, for which it had never forgiven him, though some of the less desirable had been friendly to him in a slyly joking way. He made one friend whom Mother and I both disliked, Homer Thorndike, that ne'er-do-well who drives the huckster's wagon when he feels like it and lives outside the village in a tarpaper shack. Homer comes of a good family and he's not bad-looking in a rough sort of way, but he's never been good for anything, and yet he's always had an attraction for the village boys, who like to hang around his shack. He and Tony used to go fishing together and Tony used to go off to Homer's shack for hours at a time. He said he liked to smoke with Homer.

The pale dust rose in clouds behind us as we jolted our way along the road to the station. Once I said, "Now you *will* write, every Sunday?" and he answered, "I do not like to write letters, especially in English, but I will do what I can." Otherwise we did not have much to say to each other. I felt rather silly, insisting on coming to the station, particularly as I should have to meet Mother's displeasure when I got home.

We reached the station just as the train was coming in. There was a flurry while the wheel was checked and put in the baggage car; Tony took a valise in each hand and then turned and gave me a hasty kiss, while the two or three people on the platform and several heads from the car windows looked on with interest. The last I saw of him as the train pulled out was a part of his gray suit through the window as he reached up to put a grip in the rack overhead. He did not look back or wave.

He was thankful to get away. I never doubted that. That was nearly four years ago. I have never seen him again. As I have looked back during these years, again and again, to that day, wondering if it could have been different, deciding that it could not have, I have thought until now that he went away knowing that he would not return, intending to take Mother's money not to start a business in New York but to go somewhere else and begin a new life altogether for himself. For a long while I agreed with Mother that he must have gone back to Italy; then after Grace's first visit I realized that he had been in this country but I thought that he had started his business, though not in New York, and had turned up in Philadelphia successful and laden with spoils. I felt an anger and bitterness that has been a kind of strength to me, but that is seeping away now, as I think of what Grace told me yesterday.

Evidently the facts are quite different. He went to Philadelphia once again down and out. He had returned to his church by that time and had asked the priest, Father Doyle, to help him find work, but he must have omitted to mention that he had a wife. Why? Did he think that because I was a Protestant it wasn't really a marriage at all? But he knew very well that, whatever it was from a religious point of view, legally it was a marriage. And bigamy is a crime. Or did he just want to forget the whole thing, having lost Mother's money? Was it too painful a memory at first, and then later did he just shrug it off and hope for the best? At any rate, he *had* gone to his friend Alf Brown and Alf Brown had swindled him out of the money, and in the first year, too, for there was no trace of either of them in New York a year later when I went to look for him. What did he do between then and the spring of 1893, when he met Grace in Philadelphia? What else did he try and how many defeats did he endure?

And what a strange thing that he should go and repeat the whole thing there! Out of work, any sort of job, the kind woman older than he, the room over the stable, and then again the marriage. Only I don't suppose that Grace gave herself to him first.

In all this confusion of questions and surmises one thing stands out clearly. Tony liked women older than himself: Mother; me, for he liked me if he did not love me; Grace. Even the cousin whom he went to in England, if by any chance that part of his story was true, was an older woman. I don't know what there had been in his life to turn him that way, but there must have been something. And that makes me feel now that if he had managed to achieve even a moderate success with his business, we might have had a life together that would have been bearable for us both. I could have done as well as Grace—better, for I had a son. I always thought he was resenting me for being five years older than he was, instead of a pretty young girl—though I must say he never showed any interest at all in any of the young girls in the village—but now I realize that if he could have been contented with Grace, as he evidently was, he could have been contented with me, if there had been just us. Or perhaps if I had been different it would have been possible even here in Mother's house. He could have had his furniture repair shop here too, if only we had thought of it. But with my jealousy of Mother and her contempt for me—and both were there by that time, the jealousy and the contempt, in spite of the brittle surface we maintained—and with the sullen, grinding tension that resulted, all he wanted, all he could have wanted, was to get away.

Now Tony is dead. In all this shower of arrows that has assailed me during this last month, the one of Tony's death has somehow pierced me least deeply. He was my husband. At one time I loved him, "the dear perfidious man." If the dearness has been lost in the perfidy—and it has—perhaps, as time softens harsh outlines and dims harsh colors, the perfidy may gradually disappear into the dearness. A widow can afford to take a gentler view than an abandoned wife. But if there are two widows?

May 1st

16

Tony kept his promise for a time. His letters, written on cheap paper in his too fancy hand, were never satisfactory; they were short, impersonal and evasive. After a while they stopped altogether.

There is something agonizing about watching for letters that do not come, agonizing at first and then deadening. Every day I went to the post office, for of course I was the one to go. Mother watched for letters even more eagerly than I—and much more hopefully—but she would never expose herself to the eyes of the Elders (Earl and his wife who helped him) or of the other people who might happen to be in the store at the time. Moreover she never let me skip a day, as after a time I longed to do.

"The mail is in by now, Roberta, aren't you going?"

"It's time to go for the mail, Roberta. Of course you must go. There might be something important."

"The mail, Roberta!"

I was always relieved when it was Earl Elder behind

the little grill. "Nope, nothing today," he would say indifferently. His wife Tillie with her bright sharp eyes and her quick way of talking was unpleasantly sympathetic. "No, nothing today, I'm sorry." Or, if there had happened to be an advertisement or two, a bill or an announcement of the birth of a child to one of my old classmates or a casual postcard from someone we had met on shipboard, which was all our mail amounted to, she would say regretfully, "Nothing from New York."

Once she said, "Is he sick, do you think?" "Just a very poor correspondent," I answered as confidently as I could. As time went on the comments ceased, but I was always aware of a flutter of interest when I went into the store.

If the mail chanced to be late and the store full of people lounging around waiting for it, I always knew they were watching me speculatively, wondering what had happened and how I was taking it, waiting for me to be gone so that they could talk to each other about it. If I had any purchase to make I always attended to that first and then I would say casually, "Oh, by the way, any mail for us?" It fooled no one but it was a little easier for me; the harness rubbed in another place. In time as the months rolled on, Tillie Elder would just shake her head silently as I went in.

When spring came I took little Tony with me sometimes and bought him a peppermint stick to vary the monotony. By that time no one paid any attention at all. Everybody knew that Tony had deserted me; probably it was no more than most people expected. They went out of their way to be nice to little Tony, who was at two and a half still in skirts—white nainsook dresses and petticoats which I kept immaculate; he was a beautiful baby with his curly black hair and big dark eyes, his rosebud of a mouth.

Mother kept her faith in Tony long after I had given

up. She speculated endlessly about what might have happened; worried that he might be sick; tried to convince herself that he hated to write letters, that silence meant everything was going well, that he would have written if it had not been.

"He'll just turn up some day," she would say with invincible optimism. "Some day he'll just be here and we'll forget all this waiting and strain."

At other times she would scold, "That's the trouble with men. They have no idea how hard it is for women to wait without knowing. If he would only send some word. It's really very inconsiderate of him."

Once she said in a rare moment of self-accusation, "You were right, Roberta. I should have kept some of the money back. I should never have given it all to him at once. But I thought that sometimes not having enough money right in hand can ruin everything. And I trusted him. I still trust him. I am sure there is some explanation."

She lost weight and she slept badly; her color was poor and she had developed a nervous twist to her mouth. The only thing that eased it at all for me was that Mother and I drew closer together in our common trouble; she was much less critical of me and she depended on me for sympathy and support, for a constant, receptive ear as she went over and over her hopes, her fears, her unwillingness to give up and accept the fact that Tony really was gone.

At last I said, "Mother, suppose I go to New York and look for him. Then we'll *know*—at least as nearly as we can know."

"Where would you look?"

"First I'd go to the boardinghouse that he wrote from, of course, and then the police, I suppose, and the hospitals—"

"The directories too. You could look there. Can you manage by yourself? Perhaps I had better go with you."

"Oh, Mother, I am practically thirty-five and married. It will cost twice as much if we both go." More than twice, really, for Mother always had to do things much more lavishly than I did.

So after further talk and some backing and filling on Mother's part, I went. It was late May, nearly a year after Tony had left. The peonies were in bloom and the garden was full of the cascading notes of wrens' songs. I rode my wheel to the station and left it in the station-master's office, took the nine o'clock train to Camden and the ten-fifteen to Jersey City, where I got the ferry to New York. The ferry ride was beautiful, the river blue and tipped with white here and there by a brisk cool breeze; it was full of boats, ferries, barges, some old three-masters and several steamboats, an ocean liner coming in with immigrants crowding on her decks. I wondered how many Tonys were among that mass of foreign faces. I wondered too why I could not enjoy the scene more. I knew it was beautiful but I could not feel it; I felt only my anxiety and a nagging conviction that this whole expedition was a waste of money and doomed to failure.

I went to the Astor House, where we used to stay before our trips to Europe, and I asked for the cheapest room, winning the clerk's justified scorn. Even so it was more expensive than I expected and my money lasted, though I economized on food, only three days. I am not sure I could have endured it longer, even if there had been more money; it was such humiliating and disheartening and altogether exhausting work.

The address that Tony had put on his letters was in the upper East Side, in a district that was predominantly Italian; it turned out to be not a boardinghouse, as I had thought, but a rooming house, run-down and shabby but clean, as much as I saw of it at any rate. The woman I talked to was an elderly fat Italian with very little English. At first she could not remember Tony at all, nor Alf Brown, but after I had kept on, describing him and his clothes, his valises and bicycle, all with gestures and much repetition, she exclaimed, "*Si, si*. Not here. Gone. Long time."

"Where did he go? Didn't he leave a forwarding address? Address? Letters?" I wrote on my hand, licked an imaginary stamp and dropped it into a mailbox in the air.

Comprehension went on like a light. "Ah, *si, si*." She pulled open the drawer of a rickety hat-stand in the hall, and there among an assortment of odds and ends and derelict postcards were two of my letters to Tony, very dusty and limp.

I asked if I might talk to the other lodgers but they were all out. That evening I took a cab and went back and tried again, though I felt a little nervous alone in that neighborhood, even with the four-wheeler waiting for me at the curb. It was no use anyhow. One man thought he remembered Tony but did not know where he had gone or even when he had left there.

I went to the nearest post office and then to the main post office; I tried the police, the hospitals, the directories and, in desperation, files of old newspapers at the public library. It did not occur to me till afterwards that I might have looked up button manufacturers and asked them. There was no trace of either Tony Morelli or Alf Brown. The police took my address and promised to send me word later if they found anything.

Mother met me at the door when, on the fourth day, wilted and dusty, I rode my wheel home from the station. "Nothing?" she said. She could tell from her first glimpse of my drooping shoulders as she saw me come round from the corner.

"The police have not given up. They'll let me know."

"Oh, my poor baby!"

Did she really still think of me as her baby, or was there an element of self-dramatization in her outcry? I have wondered sometimes since then, but at that moment I felt only that her thought was of me, not of herself, and I put my arms around her in a burst of love and grief, crying out in my turn, "Oh, I'm sorry, Mother, I'm sorry!" Sorry, I meant, for all the disappointment and anxiety I had brought to her from her earliest recognition that I was a homely child with no possibility of being an ugly duckling that would turn into a swan, down to this moment when I came back defeated and empty-handed.

A tug at my skirt reminded me of my own baby, deserted and fatherless, and I picked him up and hugged him till he squealed, half in delight and half in alarm.

Delia prepared a dainty supper eloquent of silent sympathy and we ate it by the light of rose-shaded candles, with little Tony in his high chair between us. At the end of the meal, with the strawberries and cream, Mother said she had a curiously tight feeling in her chest and thought she would go to bed.

It was a warning, though neither of us recognized it, and next day she felt like herself again, only a little tired. She started in at once about changing Anthony Junior's name to Kent Ewing, and after a few ineffective protests I had it done. It was, besides being an expression of Mother's desire to perpetuate the Ewing name, an outward and visible sign of an inward and—no, not spiritual and not grace—of our unspoken recognition of the fact that we had given up, that we no longer had any expectation of seeing Tony again or the money. There was no word from the New York police and we did not look for it.

We talked about Tony all day long and into the night, day after day and night after night. Only at meal times when Delia was coming in and out did we change the subject, and then it was with an effort. We followed every avenue of speculation, analyzed every aspect of Tony's character, over and over.

"I think he *must* have gone back to Italy," Mother would say again and again. "With that money he could cut quite a swathe in a Lombardy village. He could buy a little inn and live in it the rest of his life. There must be records of what ships have sailed and what passengers were on them. You didn't think of looking into that, did you?"

"How could I? It would have been like hunting for a needle in a haystack, even if I knew how to get at the records."

"I suppose we could have hired a detective. We still could."

"But that would be expensive. And what would be the use? He's gone."

"He might have gone west, of course," I would suggest in my turn. "There are all kinds of opportunities in the West for a young man."

"I can't imagine Tony in the West. It's too big for him. No, I am positive he went back to Italy, probably straight back after leaving here."

After the first few times I stopped reminding Mother that for a while at least he had written us from New York. The letters while they lasted were some evidence of sincerity, and by this time we wanted him unrelieved black. We concluded that there was no such person as Alf Brown, that Tony had invented him as well as the button factory. But then I would remember how Tony used to look at little Tony and I would cry, "I *don't* think he'd leave his son like that! He didn't care about me but I was sure he loved the baby!"

"He seemed to care about us all," Mother would counter sadly. "He seemed happy here. He and I had the kind of understanding that is very unusual between mothers-in-law and sons-in-law. He was devoted to me."

But always after her bewilderment she returned to denunciation. "He must have had this all in mind from the beginning. He must have gone through the village and seen that this was the handsomest house and laid his plans. Perhaps he watched us for several days without our knowing it. Behind that handsome face there was a ruthless schemer." Mother's eyebrows and lips would twitch. "He was handsome but there was something sinister about his good looks. He was like a face on a Roman coin but it was the face of a Nero or a Domitian." Again and again she would say bitterly, "He had nothing but kindness from us, nothing, and now he has betrayed us."

I never tried to defend him. I had no desire to. I was hurt and humiliated and it was a miserable kind of comfort to hear him blamed. Occasionally, weary of following the same tracks that had become so worn, I would say half-heartedly, "Well, it's over now. Perhaps we should just try to forget him and go on with our lives."

But Mother would answer angrily, "I can't forget what he has done to you or what I have suffered myself. I can't stop trying to understand it and to see if we could have foreseen it and forestalled it."

So I followed her lead, cravenly thankful that she spent her energies on denouncing Tony, that she did not, except occasionally by indirection, remind me that I had brought all this on myself and her by my incredible act of sensuality and weakness. Nor did I remind her that it was she who insisted on our being married, she who had trusted Tony and given him her money. These facts were too painful to admit to our thoughts, too sharp and dangerous, like double-edged swords, to use as weapons against each other; the only way we could endure our plight was by drawing together against Tony the enemy.

We talked till we had exhausted the subject and ourselves, till we were sick and tired of the very sound of Tony's name, of the mere thought of him. What we were left with in the end—and how much was it our own creation?—was a black-hearted villain, a scheming liar and thief who had insinuated himself into our home with the purpose of making his fortune by fleecing two kind and innocent gentlewomen.

And now I know that Tony himself was betrayed by his friend. Whatever his intentions toward us, he had made no fortune for himself. Black-hearted he may have been but he was inept too, and there is something pitiable about ineptitude.

Perhaps it was a good thing that Mother and I talked it all out; perhaps we purged our hearts of emotions that might otherwise have festered and poisoned us, or perhaps by harping on it in this way we whipped ourselves up to greater fury and kept our anger hot longer than it need have been. I do not know. How can one know about oneself? Are other people crystal clear to themselves? At any rate I am thankful now that we stood together in those last days, that we did not turn and rend each other.

One day, late in August of 1892 it was, Mother had the tight feeling in her chest again, and half an hour later she was gone. She was only fifty-six. Was it Tony who shortened her life or was it I?

May 2nd

17

I am thirty-seven and I have lost by death three people who were close to me, Father, Mother, Tony. Tony I lost twice and the first time, though that was not by death, was the worst. Four people if I count Cousin Alida. Not many, perhaps, but actually all the people who have been really close to me in all these years, except Kent. And what if I should lose him, voluntarily, by adoption?

He overheard part of what Grace was saying to me, understood part of what he overheard. He thinks she wants him to come and stay with her and go to school in Philadelphia, as I stayed with Cousin Alida sometimes when I was going to school. He understood very well about the cottage at Spring Lake and the children, Johnny and Helen and Ralph. They are constantly in his mind and on his tongue and even the horse is neglected. In self-defense I remind him of it, to get him away from me. He follows me everywhere, pleading, asking questions that I cannot answer, that I would not answer if I could. He even asks me about Cousin Alida and my own schooling, as if he realizes that I feel myself on less firm ground there.

"I only stayed with her once in a great while, when the weather was bad. Most of the time, practically *all* of the time, I went back and forth on the train every day. It was a long trip but I was a big girl then. When I was little I stayed at home in Ewingville and Grandmother taught me my lessons."

He gave me a dark look under his brows at that. It was plainly not a welcome thought, to stay home in Ewingville and be taught one's lessons by one's mother. "I'll stay with Auntie Grace when I'm *little* and when I'm big I can go on the train."

"No, sir, you'll stay right here with Mama."

"*Please.*"

"No, darling. It's out of the question. Now don't say anything more about it."

When I was small and was told to say nothing more, that was the end of it. I said nothing more, whatever I might think. Kent climbed into my lap—I was sitting in the sewing chair darning stockings—and wound his arms tight around my neck, breathing moistly into my ear, "*Please*, Mama."

"Look out for the needle, dear."

I hugged him back, such a strong, warm little body, smelling of small boy, pulsing with longings that I can't fulfill, my child out of my body, yet so alien, so hard to understand.

"Mama, I *want* to."

"Yes, I know. I'm sorry."

He tore himself out of my arms and flung himself face down on the floor, drumming with his feet and roaring,

104

"I don't *want* to stay in Ewingville. I want to go to school in Philadelphia and live with Auntie Grace."

"Come, Kent, get up. Don't act like a baby. Get up at once and be quiet."

But the roars turned into wails and sobs, so heart-broken that I could hardly endure it. I hoisted him by force to his feet and he flung himself down again. I tried to drag him to the bathroom to wash his face but he sat defiantly on the floor, digging his heels in. At length I left him and went down to the kitchen to make a pudding for supper. After a while he came drooping after me, hiccoughing, his face streaked, and conde-scended to lick the pan. It was raining and we could not go outdoors, so I read to him until he fell asleep. Then I tiptoed away, took the photographs of Johnny, Helen and Ralph from under his pillow where he has been keeping them, and put them in an envelope to mail back to Grace.

I wonder how Mother felt about my being with Cousin Alida as much as I was. I wonder if her bringing me home after Father's death was entirely because she thought she needed me or at least partly to get me away from Cousin Alida. I wonder how I would have felt if I had lived with Cousin Alida instead of just staying with her occasionally. As it was, there was never the slightest question in my mind as to where my love and loyalty lay. I was fascinated by Cousin Alida but I adored Mother. It would never have occurred to me that there was even a possible choice between them. But I was older than Kent.

Would Grace, I wonder, consider the possibility of having Kent stay with her and go to school—and come home week-ends? I shouldn't think she would. She wants a child she can adopt, who would be wholly hers.

She doesn't want merely to assume the school bills for someone else's child, and how could I accept such an obligation? I hate compromises anyhow. They're never satisfactory.

May 3rd

18

For two years and a little more Ned Wadsworth and I used to go to the city together on the train, when I was going to Miss Foote's and he was going to Friends Central. He would come from the west end of Main Street and I from the east end of First; we met at the corner of Main and Station Road and walked to the station, Ned carrying my books; we rode side by side to Camden and crossed the river by the Market Street ferry; there we parted, he to go on to Fifteenth and Race and I to Tenth and Spruce. He and his little brother went to Friends Central, a day school, instead of George School, a boarding school, like the other Quaker boys and girls in Ewingville. I was glad that he was the only one, for if there had been other young Friends he might not have ridden so regularly with me.

I loved those rides with Ned. He was a year older than I and a class ahead, so that I looked up to him a little and felt flattered that he noticed me. He was a plain Friend, with no style at all, and a country boy besides.

His clothes looked home-made. Beside the city boys whom I sometimes met, brothers of the girls I knew at school, Ned was all that Mother said he was, rustic, unworldly, naïf, badly dressed. She also said that he was "pious" (horrible word as she said it) but *that* he was not. He talked about his religion occasionally but quite naturally, and sometimes he joked about it in a way that might have seemed irreverent to a good Episcopalian but which to me was just his way of being natural, as if religion was part of everyday life, not something low-voiced for Sunday.

His younger brother Tommy, who was only ten or eleven, also went to Friends Central on the train, but Tommy was very independent and preferred to go alone. Sometimes we would see him scampering down the road ahead of us, jumping the puddles; sometimes he lagged behind, studying his lessons as he came and running to catch up at the last moment while Ned yelled to him to hurry and held the train for him. He would make a face at us as he scrambled in and ostentatiously sit as far away from us as he could.

Tommy was a great pet in his family, an original, whose sayings were reported with amusement. Some of them I would never have dared to repeat to Mother, she would have been so shocked, but Tommy's own family apparently never turned a hair. "Get the hell out of here!" he roared at Ned one night at bedtime. "Can't thee see I'm saying my prayers?" And another time he reproached his mother for going off somewhere without him one day when he had dawdled, with: "Why didn't thee wait for me, Mother, thee skunk, thee!" But the last I heard of Tommy, four or five years ago, he was in South Carolina, teaching Negro children in a little boarding school for Negroes run by the Quakers.

Ned was like that too, though quieter; full of life, wholly careless of any impression that he might be making, good and kind to the core of him. Fun too. And interesting. I was shy and reserved with most boys but it was easy for me to be myself with Ned.

He opened up the world of nature to me. I already loved the country around Ewingville—in all this tangle of questions about myself, the cloudy, uncertain person that I seem to be when I try to examine myself and my life, that one thing anyhow is clear: I love this land where I was born—but it was a vague, sentimental sort of love. Ned made me see the land as it was and see the other lives that shared it with me. He knew the birds, the wildflowers, the insects, the little animals of the night, opossums, raccoons, bats, foxes and skunks, the moths. He lent me books about them. The Wadsworths had plenty of books on their interests—nature, religion, history—though there were no novels in their house.

One Saturday—Seventh Day to Ned—afternoon in spring when I was fifteen, he came to the house for me, saying that he had something to show me. "And then Mother wants to know if thee'll stay for supper with us."

I went in to ask Mother but encountered Father instead. "Sure," he said. "Why not? It's very nice of Mrs. Wadsworth." He went out to speak to Ned.

"I ought to change my dress if I'm going out to dinner," I said uncertainly, torn between wanting to put on my new green dress and not wanting to keep Ned waiting. But he said, "No, come as thee is. It isn't a party. Can thee walk in those shoes?"

So I went off happily with him into the sunshine, my head bobbing along near his shoulder, taking a skipping step now and then to keep up with his long strides.

What he had to show me was a killdeer's nest in a farm lane behind the Quaker meetinghouse. It was not a proper nest at all, just a hollow in the ground right between the wagon tracks, with four speckled, cream-colored eggs in it. The hen flew off as we came up to look and Ned said we mustn't linger, but we did stay long enough to build a barrier of stones and branches around the nest so as to divert the farm wagons.

After that we went off into the woods and he showed me where there was a big patch of trailing arbutus. The flowers were past but the rough dull-green biggish leaves were there, close to the ground, and I marked the spot by a stand of tall tulip poplars so that I could go back other years when the blossoms were out. He showed me too where lady's-slippers grew and an ovenbird's nest that he had found. Ovenbirds are common enough, shouting "Teacher, teacher!" ventriloquially from the ground so that it sounds as if they were high in a tree, but the nest is so cleverly constructed and well hidden that it is very unusual to find one. I have never been able to find one myself.

As the sun was setting we went back to Ned's house, a little muddy, with twigs and bits of leaves clinging to our clothes, my hair breaking loose from its braids and hanging in tendrils—or perhaps strings is the more accurate word—about my warm, red face.

Mrs. Wadsworth took me upstairs to straighten up for supper. The Wadsworth house is older than ours. Like ours it was built of limestone, but it was what they used to call a "single" house, with windows on one side of the front door instead of both sides. We went in at the side door into a big homey sitting room behind two small parlors; the dining room was behind the sitting room and the kitchen behind that. Upstairs the spare room was over the front parlor and had a fireplace. There was a chest of drawers with wooden knobs, a bed with four chunky posts, a corner washstand with a rather battered Canton basin and ewer set, a Ware chair and an easy chair, all old but well polished. I washed in cold water from the ewer and dried my hands and face on a hem-stitched towel, combed my hair before a plain walnut mirror. The furniture was as old as ours, or older, but all plain; there was no carving, no glass knobs or brass handles, no pediments. Quaker, I decided.

Mrs. Wadsworth wore "the plain dress." She had a very sheer white muslin cap, under which her dark hair was parted in the middle and combed smoothly over her ears; her drab-colored sleeves were skimpy with no puff to them at all; her bodice plain and snug, her skirt full. She had a white fichu of sheer muslin like her cap. Her face was serene and kind, her eyes blue. She might have been pretty if she had been dressed up and had not had to wear spectacles like Ned. Only hers were gold-rimmed. Her eyes twinkled when she smiled and her manner was warm.

Ned's father was tall, like Ned; his hair was very light, lighter than his skin, which was weather-beaten, especially the back of his neck. He had a big dairy farm and he did a lot of the work himself. Like Ned he was slow of speech. He was quite courtly, though, as he made me welcome and held my chair for me at the dining-room table and pushed me in. I sat at his right, Ned and Tommy across the table. We all bowed our heads in silence, the Quaker grace.

I was seized with an almost uncontrollable desire to giggle, partly in reaction to the unaccustomed silence and partly because of what Ned had told me earlier. Tommy had done something so outrageous that morning that he had been condemned to eat his lunch alone at a small side table, though in the dining room with the family. When they all had bowed their heads, Tommy's voice broke the silence.

"Lord, I thank thee," he chirped, "for setting a table before me in the presence of mine enemies."

I safely converted a snort into a cough and the silence ended.

Dinner was delicious: roast beef and asparagus, I remember, with charlotte russe for dessert; even Father would have praised it. An old colored woman who said *thee* like the rest of them (it sounded as odd to me as a small child speaking French) waited on the table.

I remember now only two things we talked about at supper. Mr. Wadsworth said that Walt Whitman the poet had come to live in Camden; had I ever seen him?

I often saw him on the ferry going home, white-haired, white-bearded, immaculate in a gray suit and white shirt.

"Yes, he's the cleanest-looking man I ever saw," I answered and then blushed to my ears, for I thought it might sound as if I thought Mr. Wadsworth was less clean than the highest standard, which was not what I had meant at all. Mr. Wadsworth saw the blush and misinterpreted it.

"Some of his poetry would not be suitable for thee to read but some of it is very beautiful. I am particularly partial to 'O Captain, my captain.'"

He recited in his slow way,

"O Captain, my captain, our fearful trip is done,
The ship has weathered every storm, the prize
we sought is won—"

right through from the first stanza to the end of the third, when his wife interrupted gently, "Thy supper will be getting cold."

Imperturbably he finished the poem. "A great tribute to a great man," he said. "Worth a cold supper."

"Roberta, tell Father and Mother what thee told me," said Ned, "about thy memory of Lincoln's death."

They all turned expectantly toward me. I knew that Ned was showing me off, trying to put my best foot forward for his parents but I did not mind at all; I felt quite tender towards him.

"Oh. Why, I was just a little thing and very patriotic and I wanted an American flag quite dreadfully. Father and Mother went up to the Sanitary Fair in Philadelphia and they promised to bring one home to me. So when they came back I was out in the driveway to greet them, demanding my flag. Father leaned out of the carriage and handed the flag to me, tightly furled, and he said sadly, 'Here it is, but you mustn't wave it. The President has been killed.' "

After dinner we all played Parchesi with Tommy, and Ned showed me his collection of Indian arrowheads and tools that he had picked up in the fields round about. He knew a great deal about the Indians who lived here before the white men came; they were Lenni Lenape, a branch of the Algonquin tribe. He had stories about their relations with early Quakers, how the Friends used to leave their children in the care of friendly Indians when they went up to Philadelphia to their Yearly Meeting, and I told him our family story about the Indians who came for breakfast.

About nine o'clock I said my good night and thank you, and Ned walked me home through the moonlight.

"Well, did thee have a good time?" said Mother in a squeaky voice as soon as Ned was out of earshot. "Did anybody quake?"

"Oh, *Mother!*" I said.

That was the first time I went to the Wadsworths' house for a meal, but there were many other times later.

Ned was very much on my mind those days. It was

Ned I daydreamed about as I came home from school alone, a long-continued imaginary companionship that went on day after day, until Father's death put an end to school and the train trips and to the daydreaming as well, for I always felt that if I had not been in such a mazed state that day I should have been aware of his accident earlier than I was, and it seemed somehow disloyal to have been imagining Ned grown up and well dressed and acceptable to Mother bending adoringly over my hand, while Father lay in the front hall on a door with his head bloody and his pince-nez dangling.

That spring Ned graduated from school and the next fall he went to Swarthmore College, which was not far away but too far to go back and forth every day. So he lived at the college and I saw him only in the holidays. Occasionally he wrote to me, offhand, boyish letters, and at the end of the four years he invited me to his graduation, to which I went with his parents and Tommy. Mr. Wadsworth took his carriage and pair of sorrel horses, and coming back I sat squeezed in the back seat between Tommy and Ned and Ned held my hand the whole way.

Occasionally Ned came to dinner at our house but that was not so successful, especially after Father died. For one thing Mother always insisted on having at least one and preferably two other couples. "It looks better," she said. It was not easy to scare up two suitable young couples. Most of the young people went away; the others married right after school and became preoccupied with babies. I did not know any of them well. There was nobody young in our little church. So it meant much planning and discussion, often trying two or three times before we could get someone who was free—or wanted —to come. And then we were all quite shy and stiff with each other; conversation languished. I was awkward and hated it. Ned would be full of quips that fell flat. Afterwards Mother would sigh and say, "I did my best. But your beau is not very socially adept, is he?"

What I enjoyed most, except for the walks we had alone, were the expeditions we went on with a crowd of Quaker young people, including Tommy and other small boys as well as married couples: sleighing in winter, stopping at the Seven Stars for hot chocolate and waffles; huckleberrying in summer, when we hired boats in the pine barrens and rowed through the swift, silent, shady, sun-splashed waterways, with a sheet draped over the boat, shaking down the berries from the bushes that hung over the water; or sunset picnics on the bluffs above the Delaware River.

One Sunday I went to meeting with the Wadsworths. I knew the meetinghouse well from the outside, a simple brick building with a porch with a sloping roof all round it and two doors, one for the men, one for the women, but I had never been inside. It was quite plain and bare, with straight, unvarnished benches on either side of a center aisle. In the front of the room were two rows of raised benches where the "elders" sat. The men sat on the right side of the room, the women on the left. Mr. Wadsworth sat on the facing bench and ordinarily Mrs. Wadsworth did too, but that day she kept me company in the body of the meeting. Ned and Tommy were across the aisle.

There were perhaps thirty people there—I didn't like to turn my head to count—and it was amazing to me how still they all were, even the children. I have never experienced so deep a silence, and I wouldn't have thought it possible that so many people could be so quiet together. We sat for over an hour and nobody said a word. Not one word. I did not know what you were supposed to think about, so I looked at the window nearest me and thought about the tree that was framed there. It was an old white oak that grew in the graveyard next to the meetinghouse, one of the glories of our part of the country, majestic and wide-branching, with sun on its leaves, full of warblers that day. I could just see them flitting among the leaves, too far away to identify. A titmouse called "Peter! Peter!" and an oriole sang, and the warblers kept up a musical sweet chattering and cheeping. I heard the chestnut-sided warbler announce distinctly, "I want to see Miss Beecher!"

I felt strangely peaceful when the hour was over, though not holy, as I would have if I had been to church. I did wonder if I should like to do that every Sunday of my life and I thought I should miss the prayers and responses of the Episcopal service and the hymns, even though our organ was creaky and wheezy and the voices of the congregation mostly cracked and uncertain. But I don't go to church now and I don't miss it, or I seldom do. I think I miss most the walking to church as a family, Father and Mother and I, and, when I was little, Grandfather too, and the Sunday morning feeling of buckwheat cakes behind and roast chicken ahead and holiness, or perhaps only conformity, infusing all.

I dreaded trying to tell Mother what meeting was like, but she surprised me. She had gone once herself years before. "You know, I liked it," she said. "But you could never be one of them. They're born to it."

After college Ned went into the office that had been Father's, acting as assistant to the rather negative little man who succeeded Father. He never seemed to pay attention to any other girl but me, though some of the Quaker girls had come home from George School and were not married, but he never paid any very personal attention to me either. He never made me compliments, never made even the mildest kind of love to me. He

116

liked being with me, obviously; he took me for granted as he might a sister or a cousin. He was not earning enough to marry on then. Was he waiting until he had more money? Did he think of me the way I thought of him? Had he any idea at all how I thought of him, or did I hide my feelings too successfully, afraid of "taking him seriously" as Mother had once done when the man had meant nothing?

Still, they were happy and peaceful if uneventful times we had together, marred only, afterwards, by Mother's making fun of him, of his high-pitched voice, his Quaker speech, what she called his homespun interests.

"Did thee see the yellow-bellied nutcracker?" she would squeak. "Or the mouse-eating flapdoodle?"

One evening when he brought me home from a strawberry festival at the Methodist Church, he kissed me good night on the front steps and I clung to him, kissing him back. I don't know whether Mother saw or just suspected, but it was not long after that that she announced we were going abroad. It is a time-honored way of disposing of an unwanted suitor; I knew it and I suppose Ned did. But I wanted very much to go abroad and, I thought, it was only for three months and what difference could three months make?

"Why do you so dislike Ned Wadsworth?" I asked Mother once.

"I don't dislike him. He's not important enough to dislike. He's an estimable young man, I'm sure—if you like country bumpkins. Oh, he comes of a good old family, I know, and all the Quakers consider themselves the original aristocrats because they ruled this part of the country for nearly a hundred years. But he is totally unpolished. You must see that for yourself. It is so easy to slip into something without realizing it. Then suddenly you wake up and find that you are caught. I am looking for something much wider and more brilliant for you, Roberta."

We went abroad. But there was nobody interesting on the ship either going or coming and only passing acquaintances at the hotels and pensions where we stayed a few days or a week or two at a time as we progressed from Stratford to London to Canterbury, from Paris to Venice to Florence to Assisi to Rome. I loved it all—how I loved it! What I had read came alive for me; all I read afterwards was illumined by it. I got a taste for travel that is a hunger in me still. Before I go to sleep at night I often find myself walking across the fields to Anne Hathaway's cottage, or climbing the steep winding road to the Carceri, or looking out over the Piazza and the Lagoon from the top of the Campanile, and it is all as fresh and sharp as if I had been there yesterday. I dream of going back and doing it all again, of seeing places where I have not been, the Lake Country, the West Highlands, the Rigi, the Pont d'Avignon. Just the names are magic. To be on a ship's deck as the buildings of New York retreat into a skyline; to arrive at an inn in a cab at dusk, with porters and doormen emerging from a lighted doorway; to roam around a strange room which is to be home for a week or a fortnight, assessing its amenities: I love even the mechanics of travel.

But when we came home in September—a dry and dusty September, I remember—after that first trip, I found things different. Ned and I were never again on just the same easy terms. I saw him from time to time but he was also with Anna Chase a good deal. She was four or five years younger, a rosy, yellow-haired, merry little person with wide-apart blue eyes, a short upturned nose and a rather large mouth, a generous mouth. She was a birthright Friend, of course; her father was the local doctor and very much loved. It was nearly two years before they announced their engagement; I should have seen it coming but I didn't. I just wondered what had gone wrong between Ned and me.

May 5th

19

Who am I? I wrote a month or so ago. I am a woman with a problem. It is like a cancerous growth that has suddenly appeared and swelled until it seems almost that the problem is the woman.

Last Saturday Kent ran away. I did not miss him at first; I was upstairs making over my blue linen skirt into a Russian blouse for him and I thought he was in the stable playing with Dusty; I was absorbed, I suppose, and more time went by than I realized. Suddenly things seemed abnormally quiet and I jumped up and went to look for him. He was nowhere to be found.

As it was Saturday, Pete was home from school; he heard me calling Kent and came over to join in the search. I thought of the woods behind the house and then of the farm, but Pete said,

"He's always talking about his Auntie Grace. Maybe he's gone to find her." He hesitated a moment. "I didn't know you had any relations, Mrs. Morelli."

"He means Mrs. Peacock. She's not exactly a relation. Her husband was a—a kind of cousin of Mr. Morelli's." I gathered my wits together, realizing that whatever I told Pete now would be the village's permanent view of my situation. "She came to see me after Mr. Morelli died."

"Oh," said Pete, assimilating this and storing it up to tell his mother.

"But she lives in Philadelphia," I continued. "He couldn't be going to see her."

Or could he? Our eyes met. Without a word we started off hot-foot, Pete and I, for the station.

That is where he was. The ticket office was closed for the lunch hour, but Kent was sitting patiently on a bench on the platform with his piggy bank in his hands.

I did not scold him. I just took his hand and we trudged home again in silence. For a while Pete kept saying over and over, "Gee, if I'd done that when I was little I'd have got a lickin'," but soon he seemed to feel our great sadness and he too fell silent. At our gate we parted and I thanked him for his help.

In the sitting room I sat down in the rocker and took Kent on my lap and held him, rocking gently and saying nothing. He did not struggle to get free but sat there quietly for a little while, silent too. I can remember times in my own childhood when silence was the only thing that helped. Mother always belabored any point she wanted to make with scourges of words, till I was raw inside and rebellious, but Father understood the power of a sympathetic silence. That time he caught me in a fib and all he said was, "I didn't think you would. You've always been so truthful." And then on some pretext or other he kept me with him while he worked, without talking, till I was calm and contrite.

That afternoon, Saturday, I took Kent out to the farm. The farm collie had had a litter of pups and Mrs. Duchamps offered us one. I told Kent that when the puppy was big enough to leave its mother he could have it, and the light came into his eyes again.

More bricks had fallen from the chimney of the house, and Mr. Duchamps told me that something really would have to be done about it. I told him that I had the estimates and that I would decide at once.

I had had them two weeks or more and just had not faced them. The first was for $87, the second a flat $100. It does not make much difference which it is for I haven't got either. I have $37.56 in the savings bank and a little more in my checking account, but we can't use that for that is all there is to live on until the first of July. I already have a bill at Elder's store and my taxes on the house and farm both are long overdue.

After two sleepless nights I decided that I would have to sell some of the Ewing glass. It is valuable, I know. The South Jersey glassmakers made mostly window glass and bottles of all shapes and sizes, but they all made some things for their own use besides. In the Ewing glassworks there was a workman from Rotterdam who was a talented glass blower and etcher, and he made the elegant goblets, tumblers, vases and so forth that the family used for a century and more, much of which I still have.

I spent some time on Tuesday taking it all down, looking it over, making up my mind what I could bear to give up. Not the goblets. I have too many memories of our dinner parties and the confident, easy life we lived then to want to part with them. Besides I use them myself sometimes and I want to hand them on someday as a complete set to Kent's wife. The candlesticks of aquamarine glass with a sapphire saucer base, which are very pretty, I could spare much more easily, but I wondered if they would sell. The sugar bowl with the swan finial is a lovely thing, but the matching creamer is gone. I remember the shocking day Kate broke it; it just came to pieces in her hands, she said. A set of something would be the best, I thought, and I hesitated between the nine tumblers and six tall pale-green wineglasses with twisted stems and bowls etched with thistles. In the end I packed the wineglasses carefully into the old carpetbag. The tumblers were older and heavier; we used to use them for every day, but I can't ever remember using the wineglasses. Father was a teetotaler.

I added a miniature pitcher with a tiny ball cover and lily pad decoration made of clear flint glass and hesitated over the flip-flop. I well remember Grandfather's putting his lips to the ribbed stem and the bowl's giving out a series of small, sharp booms—exciting to a child, but a dangerous toy, for too big a puff might break the diaphragm and even draw bits of glass into the blower's lungs. I was never allowed to touch it, and I am always afraid that Kent will go experimenting with it some day. But I can't imagine anyone's wanting to buy it now, even as a curiosity, and so I put it back. I took instead an amber vase about seven inches tall with darker handles, which I've never cared especially about.

This morning, after leaving Kent with Esther Snaith as I had arranged to do, I went off to Philadelphia with my precious load. I went straight to Healy's in Chestnut Street, where Cousin Alida used to deal.

I had to wait quite a while before I was attended to. The clerk did not think me impressive-looking in the first place, and after he had learned that I had come to sell, and not to buy, he was even more indifferent, but at last I was taken into a little office in the back, where a Mr. Thompson came to talk with me. He was much more polite and quite excited, though he tried to hide it, when he saw what I had brought with me.

He bought all of it. He paid me five dollars apiece for the wineglasses, twenty dollars for the vase, and to my surprise twenty-five dollars for the miniature pitcher, which he handled as if he could hardly believe it. He kept taking the little ball cover off and fitting it back again. No doubt they were all worth more and he will sell them for twice what he paid me, but I have enough now to fix the chimney and I don't intend to sell any more glass, though Mr. Thompson urged me to come back again, after his suggestion that he come down to Ewingville to look at my glass himself met with no response.

In spite of my fat pocketbook I felt very hollow and guilty as I came away from Healy's with my lightened carpetbag, as if I had betrayed my ancestors and defrauded Kent, but at least I can afford to pay Dixons the hundred dollars and it is probably worth the thirteen dollars' difference for they are better and more reliable workmen, Mr. Duchamps says. For the moment money is not my problem, though it will be before long, for I can't meet all emergencies by selling off Kent's inheritance bit by bit.

The city has changed a great deal in the twenty years since I used to go to school there. The horsecars are gone. Now there is a trolley car on every street, down Chestnut, up Walnut, down Spruce, up Pine, up Thirteenth and down Twelfth, both ways on Market and Broad. The open trolleys were already on for summer and I must say it is very pleasant riding and swaying along in the fresh air, especially when you are lucky enough to get an end seat. I must take Kent to the city for a treat—but then he would insist on seeing Auntie Grace.

After I had disposed of my pieces of Ewing glass, I walked down Chestnut Street to Twelfth to look at Penn Charter School, not to go in but just to look. It stands on the corner of Twelfth and Market and next door to it is an old red brick Friends Meeting House with its end to the street and two white porticoes on the south side facing a grass plot with trees. It looked old and peaceful and quiet in the midst of the busy city clatter of drays, carriages, trolley cars and bicycles. The school, also a plain, substantial brick building, is to the north of it, and I believe that one day a week the boys are all lined up and marched into the meetinghouse to attend a Quaker meeting. I should like to see it, but this was evidently not the day. I did see in the yard between the buildings, which is protected by a high iron fence, a class of little boys doing calisthenics with a teacher, such nice, open-faced little boys with a look of breeding.

From there I went to look at the Episcopal Academy at Locust and Juniper, a Tudor building in brown stone, very English-looking. I saw a gentleman go in with a carnation in his buttonhole and carrying a cane, a father, I suppose, gone to confer about his son. On the whole I liked the looks of Penn Charter better, but both of them were a far cry from the drab little public school in Ewingville, with its privies out back and the mixed lot of youngsters inside: some children from near-by farms, some middle-class Ewingville children, old Moses's grandchildren, the junkman's tattered brood and the dull, apathetic offspring of Loreen Daly, who lives in a hovel at the far end of the village and takes in washing—and other things.

After I left the Episcopal Academy I walked down one block to Spruce and past Cousin Alida's house. It looked just as it always did, except that the doors and shutters and window trim had been painted cream color instead of white, not an improvement. Miss Foote's School has been moved farther west and I did not see that.

Instead I walked up to Broad Street and took the trolley north to Grace's house. I felt I had to see it, for houses do tell you something about the people who live in them. On the way, at the corner of Broad and Race, we passed the Catholic High School, a handsome, almost new building—the date carved over the door was 1889—all in white marble, and it occurred to me that this, rather than Penn Charter or Episcopal Academy, was the school that Kent really would go to in the end when the time came, supposing that it did come, which of course it won't. It was so much more convenient to Grace's house, and anyhow why should a Catholic boy attend Penn Charter—and he would be a Catholic boy. Perhaps Penn Charter would not even take him.

I got out at Girard Avenue and walked half a block under Norway maples. I was taking a chance, I knew, walking past Grace's house. Suppose she looked out of a window and caught me. But it was as if I were driven to do it, and not just by vulgar curiosity either. I felt oddly déclassée walking past her house and looking up at it, estimating it, as if I were a kind of spy or a poor relation assessing the prospects. I wondered how Tony felt in the same circumstances, looking at our house, looking at Grace's, making up his mind. How many other houses did he inspect before he settled on those two, I wonder? I am sure he was more impressed by Grace's; it is far more opulent—and yet his taste was simple enough to appreciate our old furniture, even the oldest and plainest of it.

Grace's house is not as I imagined it; it is grander and still more hideous. More house and less ground. It resembles that monstrosity of a summer cottage that she showed me the picture of, but it is larger and, being all in stone and brick and marble instead of wood, it is more overwhelming. There is an even more imposing double staircase going up to a sort of loggia across the front, and topping the whole edifice, above and around the third-story windows, is a sort of false front—I don't know the architectural term—shaped like the top of the façade of the church of San Miniato on the hill outside Florence.

I stood and looked as long as I dared, revising my first ideas of it, trying to see it as Tony first saw it. He had not come there successful and confident as I had imagined. Possibly he had worn the gray suit in which he left Ewingville, but it must have been shabby by that time. He had come here defeated, suffering from the shock of his partner's betrayal of him. His friend Alf Brown had meant a great deal to him; he always spoke that undistinguished name with warmth and admiration in his voice, as if he were speaking of someone generally acknowledged to be important. To have Mr. Brown defraud him of the money and desert him must have been bitter indeed. For the first time I felt a little sorry for him.

He had gone back to his church and he approached Grace's great pile of a house with the encouragement and approval of the priest. That in itself must have been almost as much of a defeat as a support; he used to be very irreverent about Mother Church and to regard all religion as a convenient hocus-pocus for keeping the poor and ignorant quiet, much as you give a pacifier to a fretful baby.

I wondered if he climbed the high steps to the front door or went around by the little path along the side of the house to the back, and what he said to the maid who answered his ring. Or perhaps he hung around until he saw Grace come out and spoke to her directly.

127

There was no room beside the house for a driveway to the stable, of which I got a glimpse, its rooster weather vane winking in the sun. It must have been entered from a back alley. Perhaps Tony had the sign of his furniture repair shop in the alley. I could not imagine it attached anywhere on that grandiose front. But I reminded myself that Grace worked with him in partnership; they had been planning to move to a shop in Spring Garden Street.

Mother and I had seen what he could do with furniture and how he transformed our own discarded pieces, but it had not occurred to us that he had a talent which could be used to give him employment and to make money. He could just as well have had a furniture repair shop in Ewingville as in Philadelphia; if there weren't so many people to come to it, still the word would have got around the countryside. He could have moved to the county seat as well as to Spring Garden Street. But Grace had a grasp of practical things, a business acumen that was entirely lacking in us. We could not think in terms of small beginnings near at hand, only in terms of a vague investment in New York. If we had been more keen, more practical, more down to earth, everything might have been different.

This is what I was thinking as I turned back towards Girard Avenue to get the trolley. Engrossed, I did not see Grace coming. I did not even recognize her when I came face to face with her. It took her exclamation, "Why, Roberta! What luck! I might have missed you!" to make me realize that contrary to all my intentions I had run smack into her. Served me right, of course, for snooping.

She was wearing a black linen suit with a lace-encrusted shirtwaist and the black straw hat with the shiny wings that I had seen before. She looked hot, or perhaps she was only flushed at seeing me. But her delight sounded genuine, and I pretended as she swept me along with her that I really had come intending to call and was going away disappointed. I hoped that the maid would not betray the fact that I had not rung the doorbell, but the question did not arise. Grace let herself in with her latchkey and then summoned the maid to tell her to bring us some lemonade.

All this time I had been carrying my carpetbag. It was not heavy, with the glass gone, and it did not bother me at all until I met Grace. It is strange how plebeian it makes you feel, not so much to *carry* a parcel or a piece of luggage as to be *caught* doing it. I set it down as unobtrusively as possible in the hall inside the door. I saw Grace look at it with curiosity but she did not say anything and I didn't either. "Never explain," Mother used to say.

It was all as different as possible from her first visit to me. She did not take me into her parlor, though I had a glimpse of it between gold-fringed velvet portières as we went by; it screamed money. Instead she led me into a large airy room which she called the morning room. Somewhat to my chagrin it was charming: bright with cretonnes and bowls of roses, filled with simple, comfortable modern furniture and with evidences of a variety of interests: an elegant little sewing table of the kind I have always wanted, an upright piano, a small desk with pigeonholes stuffed with letters, even a mahogany bookcase containing not rows of sets but books that looked as if they had been chosen to read—Kipling, R.L.S., *The Little Minister*, Owen Meredith's *Lucile*. There were photographs everywhere, a plethora of babies, dressed and undressed, and small children with sunbonnets and sand pails and spades; some cabinet photographs of older people, her parents, a formidable-looking man who might have been her first husband—and Tony. It must have been an enlarged snapshot of Tony, for he was sitting on a verandah railing, wearing white tennis clothes and laughing. He looked extraordinarily handsome, very relaxed and at ease, and young. A knife turned in my heart.

"Goodness, it's gotten hot!" Grace took off her hat and jacket and flung them onto the sofa, from where the capped and aproned maid, after setting down the tray of refreshments, retrieved them and took them away. I had forgotten to get any lunch and I realized, sipping the iced lemonade and biting a crisp, delicate sand tart, that I was starved.

"This is such a nice surprise," Grace babbled. "I've been looking for some word from you every day, so I shouldn't be surprised, should I? I'm not, really, I'm just pleased. Do have another cookie, there's nothing to them."

"They're delicious," I murmured, and took a third. I was ashamed but I couldn't help it. I was so hungry.

"Have you been to see Mr. Kirkpatrick?" said Grace eagerly.

"Mr. Kirkpatrick?" For the moment I was wholly at a loss as to whom she meant.

"My lawyer. I gave you his address. No, I see you haven't. Oh, dear, I so hoped you had been. He knows about you and is expecting you. He can tell you all about me so much better than I can myself."

"That picture of Tony," I said, as if the words were jerked out of me. "When was it taken?"

"Last summer at Spring Lake." Her eyes filled up with tears and overflowed. She fumbled for a handkerchief tucked in her waistband. "I'm sorry. I didn't mean to cry. But we were so happy. I never imagined—" She wiped her eyes determinedly, set the picture to the back

130

of the table and brought out a silver-framed photograph of a round-eyed, solemn child just past the baby stage. "This is my little boy Roland. It was taken just six weeks before he slipped away from me. If you've finished—sure you won't have any more lemonade or another sand tart?—come upstairs with me. I want to show you Roland's room."

It was a large corner room with a southeastern exposure. There is no better exposure than that; you get the sun all morning but you avoid the flat western afternoon sun, which is hot and glaring and depressing. I am like Mariana of the moated grange: I most loathe the hour when the sun is sloping down the western sky. The room was decorated for a baby, with Mother Goose figures on the walls and painted furniture in small sizes; there was a soft thick carpet on the floor with a white bear rug before the well-screened corner fireplace. Through a half-opened door I could see a bathroom that looked as cool and pretty as a bowl of water lilies.

"I would re-do it for Kent, of course," Grace was saying. "This is a baby's room and he is ready for something quite masculine, with a desk and bookcases. He could be happy here, don't you think?"

"I didn't come here to give him to you."

"I know. I realize that. You just came to look me over. If I'd known you were coming, I'd have arranged for Father Doyle to be here to meet you, and my mother. But I'm glad you came anyhow."

An idea that I had rejected two or three weeks ago came back to my mind, and impulsively I blurted it out.

"How would you feel about a compromise? If Kent were to live with you in the winter and go to school but came back to me for the summer and the holidays?"

A light leaped in her eyes and I felt a moment of

panic, thinking she was going to jump at my unthought-out suggestion and I would find myself committed. But she shook her head.

"No," she said with decision. "It wouldn't work. I want a child who would be all my own. Besides it wouldn't be good for Kent at all. He would have two mothers and he would inevitably be pulled to pieces between us. But please think more about my offer."

I realized that her eyes had lit up because she thought I had given a sign of weakening.

"You are very generous and you have a great deal to give to some child—but not my boy. I can't, really I can't."

The light had gone from her eyes now, but her lips continued to smile. "Don't say it now. Wait a little longer."

Saying that I must get the afternoon train, I retrieved my carpetbag and fled. I was tired to death when I reached the ferry. I went and sat inside instead of standing out on front with my face to the breeze and the river smell as I always used to do. Walt Whitman was not on it. He has died, I think I heard. In the cavernous train shed in Camden as I got on the train on the left-hand side of the platform I remembered the old tag that I used to think so witty, "If you go to the left you're right; if you go to the right you'll be left." Such odd flotsam gets washed up on the beach of one's memory. I settled down on the hot, cinder-gritty red plush seat, and there I was with my problem sitting in my lap, buzzing in my head, swelling in my heart.

I began then to think about the unthinkable.

May 10th

20

No, I won't do it. It is preposterous. Nobody could expect me to.

She is sweet and kind; she is rich; she wants him.

I am sour and unkind; I am poor; he is mine.

May 11th

21

Grace	Roberta
Expensive hideous house	Beautiful, crumbling ancestral home
Summer cottage at Spring Lake	Occasional days at the farm
Private school	Ewingville public school, Exeter high school
A good university	Working his way through some inexpensive college
Companionship of ready-made cousins	Loneliness
Stimulation of city life	Life in stagnant village where his mother has no friends

Easily expressed affection	Inarticulate love
Wealth	Poverty
Devout Catholic	Nothing

May 12th

22

Would it have been better or worse for me if Cousin Alida had adopted me and brought me up? If, that is, she had taken me when I was Kent's age, for when I was older I would have clung to Mother.

Looking at it quite coldly, I think it would have been better. At any rate, I would have been different now. I would have been one of three things: (a) married to some Philadelphia man; (b) a schoolteacher—she believed that girls should be educated to support themselves; (c) a rich old maid, for she would probably have left her money to me instead of to the Pennsylvania Historical Society. I should have missed all the years with Mother and our love for each other, which was an intense and beautiful thing, perhaps, but also a painful one.

If I asked Kent now whose little boy he would rather be, mine or Auntie Grace's, he would choose Auntie Grace without a moment's hesitation.

You can't leave it to a child to decide.

May 13th

23

What has happened to my religion? I wrote two or three days ago that I have none and this is true.

As a child I liked to go to church and Sunday School. St. Thomas's was an extension of home. Father was a vestryman and passed the plate on Sundays. Mother was the chairman of the Altar Guild—in fact she *was* the Altar Guild—and arranged the flowers and polished the altar brasses on Saturday. The stained-glass window in the chancel—an ugly, sickly one I realize now, but I thought it beautiful then—was given in memory of the Judge by his two younger sisters, Great-aunt Ellie and Great-aunt Caroline, who always rustled into the front pew at the last moment and knelt for the conventional few seconds before sitting down. Dr. Herbert, our gentle, round-faced, white-haired, radiant rector, was often at our house, always for Sunday dinner. He was a widower who lived alone in the rectory, cared for by a housekeeper who was a notoriously poor cook. At Miss

Foote's I learned that to be an Episcopalian was socially preferable, and I felt a little complacent about that.

When I suffered what I suppose are the usual adolescent doubts, I took them with some confusion and embarrassment to Dr. Herbert, who not only reassured me as to the existence of God—and I don't suppose I really question the existence of God now, only His relevance to my life and the kindness of His church—but he made me feel that I was all the better and stronger for my questionings. " 'There is more faith in honest doubt,' " he quoted, " 'believe me, than in half the creeds.' " And again, " 'Thou wouldst not have sought Me if thou hadst not already found Me.' " His was a clear, sweet, loving spirit and I often wish that I could talk to him now. "Don't worry," he would say, "your heavenly Father knows whereof you have need; He does not let one sparrow fall to the ground; He will not fail you." And perhaps I should believe it, even now, if I heard his warm, rich voice uttering the words. And he would say, no doubt, "Keep your child, my dear. The Lord gave him to you. He will take care of you both."

But Dr. Herbert died before Tony came to Ewingville, and in his place we had a raw, stiff young man who obviously regarded Ewingville as a way station on the road to better things. He was unmarried—it was whispered that he had been blighted in love—and about my age. Quite openly he looked on me as a menace and put up every possible barrier to protect himself. He could not have made it plainer if he had worn a sign KEEP OFF! We very soon stopped inviting him to Sunday dinner because his discomfort as he cast wildly about for excuses was palpable. He was no answer to a maiden's prayer, goodness knows, with his flat nose and bad breath, and I could never become predatory about a man who said, "Between you and I—" but his vanity protected him from self-knowledge. Now that is catty. Besides, what self-knowledge is my own vanity protecting me from?

When Mother told him that Tony and I were engaged, his relief was ludicrous, and he married us with great enthusiasm in the "very quiet ceremony" which was necessary, Mother told him, because of the recent death of Great-aunt Ellie. Great-aunt Caroline, well into her eighties, came to my wedding in her best bonnet, very fragile and quite luminous over dear Roberta's happiness. She almost made me believe in it myself.

We were married in the church at four o'clock on August 1st, and besides Mother and Great-aunt Caroline the only guests were Esther and John Snaith. I protested against inviting them, for though they had lived next door to us for several years they were only acquaintances and inclined to gossip. But that was just why they must be asked, Mother said. They belonged to the church, too. After the ceremony we all walked back to the house and had ice cream and cake and Tony produced a bottle of wine.

I had wanted to go off quietly with Tony to a justice of the peace somewhere and have it done and then have Mother announce that we had been married in February, but Mother insisted that nobody would believe that, having seen Tony about the place as our hired man and nothing more all these months, and that we would be a laughingstock.

"It's always better," she said, "to carry things off with a high hand. Besides, Roberta, surely you want to be married in church?"

Kent was born on December 10th in the Judge's big bedroom over the library, which Tony and I moved into after our honeymoon, I from my small bedroom opening out of Mother's and Tony from the little rooms over the stable. Dr. Chase delivered the baby and, though he could not have been kinder or more matter of fact, that was just one more added turn of the screw of mortification.

Great-aunt Caroline, already almost detached from this world, believed until the day of her death several months later that the baby was only a little premature, but our rector could count on his fingers as well as anybody. He was outraged. He thought I had made a mock of the church and of him. He came while I was still in bed and told me so in bitter, scathing words. God, he implied, would back him up in everything he said.

I suppose it was then that I lost my religion. Perhaps God had never been very real to me, only St. Thomas's Church and Dr. Herbert. I thought sometimes of Jesus's writing on the ground with his finger and saying, "Let him that is without sin among you cast the first stone," but even Jesus had cried out at the end, "My God, my God, why hast thou forsaken me?"

To my surprise Tony insisted on the baby's being baptized, with Alf Brown for an absentee godfather, but that was the last time we any of us went into the church, except for Great-aunt Caroline's funeral. And for Mother's, three years later, but by that time we had no rector of our own; Mr. Van Doren came over from Exeter. Mother withdrew her support; no more flowers for the altar, no more little envelopes for the collection plate. Even before Tony left, our rector was gone, called to a church in Newark. I heard later that he was quite well liked there and married the daughter of a parishioner who had a prosperous shoe store.

St. Thomas's has not had a rector since. Without the contributions of the great-aunts and Mother and several others who have died, the church can't afford even the pittance it used to pay. Dr. Herbert had private means.

The Snaiths have joined the Methodist Church, and for most of the time St. Thomas's is closed. Once last summer a minister came from Camden and there was a service attended by a handful of people, of whom I was not one.

I have taught Kent to say "Now I lay me down to sleep" and ask God to bless those he loves, who now include Auntie Grace and Dusty as well as the Duchampses and, of course, Mama. Once conscientiously I tried to give him some religious instruction but he broke away from me impatiently, saying, "I know all about God. He comes and gets the Snaiths' garbage for his pigs." Just what he meant by that I wasn't able to fathom, being at the moment dissolved in laughter and struggling to hide it.

If there is a God, He must find me utterly unrewarding.

May 16th

24

That young minister. I suppose I have been quite unfair to him. I haven't thought of him for a long time, have shoved him out of my mind because the memory of him was in a small prickling way painful.

His name was Alexander Grant Wallace, and Mother and I made many a private joke about "our triple conqueror" before he arrived and even more after he came, when his mild appearance made his name seem even funnier to us. He was born and reared in Camden, started out in life as a sewing machine salesman, received a call to the ministry, studied at the Divinity School in Philadelphia and came to Ewingville to his first cure at thirty, which was just my age at that time.

I made fun of his name—"three great military heroes, no less!"—before he came, but I daydreamed about him too, long, continued-from-day-to-day, romantic imaginary scenes in which a handsome young minister, strong and tender and spiritual, looked deep into my eyes and saw there the beauties of soul that had been hidden from less perceptive mortals. Even before he came to preach his trial sermon we had, in the delicious fantasies spun at night before I went to sleep or in the library while I turned the pages of a book automatically, progressed to the point of calling each other Alex and Bobby. I squirm, writing it now, but this is purgation.

True, when he came for that trial sermon on a winter Sunday, gray and raw with snow in the air, his looks were a disappointment. He was under middle height, his nose was flat, his smile nervous, his chin negligible. His voice was surprisingly good, however, and when he raced through the service, as Episcopal ministers do, coming in on the new verse of the psalm while the congregation is still hurrying to finish the old one, he did it in tones that were rich and musical and, yes, authoritative. It must have been his voice that won him such encomiums from the Divinity School, for his sermon, aside from the compelling tones in which it was read, was only mediocre. But it was his singing of the hymns that made me forgive him his uninteresting looks and restore him to my daydreams after only a momentary lapse. He sang the old stand-bys—"The Son of God Goes Forth to War" and "Oh Jesus Thou Art Standing"—in a clear sweet baritone, not dragging or unctuous but joyous, as if he were alone with God, as if he had just at that moment composed both words and music to express his rapturous devotion. And when he sang,

> *"Art thou weary, art thou languid,*
> *Art thou sore distrest?*
> *Come to Me, saith One, and coming*
> *Be at rest"*

he did it so sympathetically, so tenderly, so warmly that I was ready to come to him forthwith. By the time that he called at our house for his first parochial visit, I had

143

reached the stage in my daydreams where I was composing his proposal every night in a different and more delightful form. How *could* I have been so abysmally silly?

I was upstairs sewing that day when he came to call for the first time. I have always liked clothes and I have never been like some homely women who give up and wear any old thing or adopt an easy uniform and drop the whole matter. Some of the worst squabbles that Mother and I got into were over my clothes; she wanted to dress me in blue because that was her color and she thought it the only one, whereas I knew that beiges and bittersweets and leaf browns brought out the color of my hair and eyes.

"With your sallow skin," she used to say, "you should wear clear colors."

"My skin isn't sallow," I would retort angrily, "it's pale, which is quite different, and if you would let me use that rouge I bought in Paris—"

"Rouge, Roberta," she would finish the argument coldly, "is the mark of a prostitute."

I never used more than just the faintest film of it, and it did make a difference.

I was sewing the day Mr. Wallace came for the first time, working on a dress made of really lovely plaid taffeta, white and gold and green and brown. It wouldn't go right—it was so difficult to match the pattern—and I was tired and frazzled when Delia came up to tell me that the new minister was downstairs and Mother said to come right away. I jumped up, hustled into my favorite olive-green broadcloth that I got in Paris, dabbed at my untidy hair with the brush and, in a last-minute frenzy to improve the unimprovable, I used some of the forbidden rouge, in my haste putting on too much and not evenly at that.

144

Mother had got off to a good start with the new rector. They were talking about Thomas à Kempis when I burst in. Mother said afterwards that she couldn't imagine what had possessed me, that I looked positively crazy, with my hair like a hurrah's nest and that rouge on my face, that I gushed all over the poor man, telling him how wonderful I thought his voice was, that I wasn't like myself at all and that I must have scared Alexander Grant Wallace almost out of his wits. I was bitterly ashamed and I think that I was never at ease with him when I saw him afterwards, nor he with me.

I wrote of him unjustly yesterday, but that is the more comfortable way in which I have come to think of him if I have to think of him at all. It is curious that sometimes it seems less painful to face one's sin than one's folly, less grievous to accept humiliation than mortification.

May 17th

25

Tony and I did have a honeymoon. Mother gave us the money for a week at Cape May. She also gave Tony money for a trousseau, for his clothes were certainly not suitable for a son-in-law of hers. He went up to Philadelphia a few days before we were married and bought them off the peg, since there was not time enough to go to a tailor. He didn't think in terms of tailor-made clothes anyhow. If he looked a little fancy and foreign in his new clothes he was quite unconscious of the fact and well pleased with himself. He was handsome enough to carry off—almost—the width of his pin stripes, the brightness of the dark blue, the pointedness of his lapels, the smallness of his waist; it was his exuberance more than his appearance that made me squirm a little inwardly.

The bride had no trousseau; she wore her old clothes, which were beginning to be a little tight. I felt elderly and drab beside my effulgent young husband and I saw, or thought I saw, curious glances directed at us.

Still, we had a happy week. We really did. I did, and I think—I am sure—Tony did too. He was gay, he was charming, he was attentive. Perhaps he was just playing a role for the benefit of onlookers in the hotel—and himself too—but if he was he played it well, in private as well as in public. But I cannot think it was only a role, for his high spirits were genuine.

My spirits rose to meet his. After all the anguish of the previous months I felt as if an enormous weight had been lifted off me. For the first time in my life, too, I was out from under Mother's thumb and the realization was heady. No longer the plain, unmarried daughter trailing along behind a beautiful mother, I was Mrs. Morelli, a bride, and the clerk at the desk, the waiters, the chambermaids and the other hotel guests to whom we talked all had a lightly deferential, even a cherishing, attitude that was like balm.

Furthermore, I was less homely than at any other time in my life. Happiness brightened my eyes and deepened their color. Pregnancy is becoming to some women and it was to me; it softened my angles, blunted my features a little, flaring my nostrils and deepening the hollows of my eyes. The moist salt air brought a wave to my hair and a bloom to my skin. The knowledge that I loved and the belief that I was loved gave me a freedom, a confidence, an élan that I had never had before. I knew all this about myself, for the hotel was full of large gilt-framed mirrors and I studied myself in them, seriously and openly when I was alone, surreptitiously when Tony was there or in the public rooms where other people were. Sometimes unexpectedly in the drawing room or the dining room I would catch sight of my reflection and for an instant not recognize myself. Then I would toss my head and exclaim inwardly, "Why, it's you!" I felt as if I were living in a miracle.

For I did love Tony and for a little while I did believe that he loved me. Incredible now in the light of his later surly indifference, his desertion, his bigamy. But why should I say or think it was not love, even though it was so soon and ingloriously over? Does the spoon cease to be silver just because it is black with tarnish? For a time, which was longer than just the week of the honeymoon, I knew what some people never know: I knew the deep rich happiness of married love.

I drank the potion more eagerly than Tony did; I know it now and I suppose I knew it then, though I did not acknowledge it to myself. It did not seem to matter anyhow. We were one, and if my overflow filled his lack, there was no need to say which was more and which was less.

We stayed at the Congress Hall, an L-shaped wooden structure with columns to the roof on two sides. Two or three South American ambassadors were summering there with their families and their carriages, and it was all very gay and fashionable. Every morning at eleven o'clock there was dancing in the ballroom and again in the evenings. In the afternoons some people went in bathing in the ocean, others rode in their carriages up and down Beach Drive or strolled on the boardwalk. In the evenings before the dancing began, people made up tables of whist in the card room.

Tony and I hired bathing suits and took dips in the surf, holding each other's chilly wet hands and jumping up and down when the breakers rolled in. We waltzed morning and evening, and several of the embassy secretaries asked me to dance while Tony whirled their wives around. Once or twice we were invited to join a whist game but afraid of losing money we declined, and it was soon accepted that the b. and g. liked to be alone on the boardwalk at sunset.

Because the bay joins the ocean just there and the bay itself is so wide, Cape May is the only place along the whole eastern coast of the United States, I suppose, where you can see the sun set over the water. We would walk all the way to the end of the boardwalk and stand there watching the sun sinking down, the "patens of bright gold" dancing on the water, until the light came on in the lighthouse; then we would turn and walk in the opposite direction, and soon see the moon rising out of the eastern sea.

"America is mostly ugly," said Tony, "but this is beautiful."

"Ugly! Oh, no!" I protested, all my love of country outraged. I felt wounded, as if he had struck me. "Tony, America *isn't* ugly!"

"Why do you disagree with part of what I say, when you can agree with the rest of it? I also said *this* was beautiful."

He was laughing and I laughed too, but I could not drop the subject. "Ewingville is not Florence," I conceded, "but it is a little beautiful too, isn't it, in its own way, when the apple blossoms are out and then in the fall when the leaves of the trees are scarlet and gold?"

"Yes, a little. But you have not seen Como yet. Some day I will take you to Lake Como."

And it seemed as though the future stretched like a straight road ahead, golden in the sunshine.

At night we lay folded in each other's arms in the white-painted, thin-mattressed wooden bed, the moonlight pale in the room and the sound of the surf swelling and falling in our ears. I wondered sometimes if it was good for the baby, but Tony said it was all right.

The day our week came to an end and we left to return to Ewingville, Tony bought me a box of chocolates to celebrate, he said, our first anniversary. Our first real one, when we had been married a year, he forgot, and by the time the second one came around he had been gone nearly two months. What went wrong? Why did it end the way it did?

Mother said that he did not respect me because of the way I had made myself cheap, the ease with which he had got me in the first place. I don't often think of that day because it never ought to have happened; but it did happen, and because it did I sit here night after night looking for someone named Roberta Morelli.

It was March and I was thirty-one. March is a bad month, the longest month in the year, I think, and the dreariest. It is cold, wet, windy. Some of our worst snowstorms have come in March, at the end of winter when everybody is tired of snow and woodpiles and coalbins are getting low. In the early part of the month there is less color than at any other time of the year. In November, for instance, which is usually considered a gloomy month, there is lovely muted color, subtle violets and russets that gradually fade out or are buried in snow. But in March the landscape is all black and dingy brown or black and dirty white. The dark clouds pile up in the gray sky and the light beneath them is somber. Or if the sun does happen to be out, it is bright and hard with not a shadow to soften its merciless glitter. Then the buds begin to swell and a faint rosiness creeps over the bare woods and now and then a mild moist day sneaks in to unsettle all your thoughts and stir up your feelings, but like as not it is only a prelude to another snowstorm.

For months and months I had been struggling against a weight of depression that covered me like a blanket, a feeling that life was passing me by, that time was moving faster and faster and leaving me behind, unneeded, unused, unwanted. Even books lost their power to take

me away and change my thoughts. I stopped reading
novels and travel books and read only poetry, in which I
found plenty to confirm me in my feelings of desolation
and rejection. All I could see lying before me were
Marvel's "deserts of vast eternity," and night after night
I lay awake and thought like Sappho,

> *Midnight. The moon has set*
> *and the Pleiades. Time passes*
> *and I lie alone.*

After Tony came I had a new interest and I found
many reasons for going to the stable, where I watched
him working over his furniture, and many opportunities
to make conversation with him. At first I think I was
scarcely conscious of what I was doing; he was a distraction, and not much more than that, from the pressure of
my empty life and my constant preoccupation with it;
but as the weeks crawled by, his dark eyes and flashing
smile, his soft, comforting voice with the hint of laughter in it, his hands, took up residence in my mind.

In February I had come down with a bad cold, the
juicy kind that makes eyes and nose stream; later it went
down into my chest and bubbled and barked in my lungs.
Mother said I was disgusting to be with and she alter-
nately scolded and shuddered. It hung on into March.

Then Cousin Alida died, quite suddenly, though she
had for a long time been ailing. But she had not been
any worse than usual; there had been no reason to send
for us. One morning when Martha, her maid who had
been with her so long, went in to wake her, she found
her dead. Martha sent Mother a telegram, which came
as a shock to me and a grief.

I had been very fond of Cousin Alida and I would
have liked to see her again before she died, to say good-

by to her. She had been an important part of my life, a touch with a wider world, a somewhat romantic figure, a source of warmth, a suggestion of freedom. She and Mother had had an often uneasy relationship and from time to time I had been aware of friction between them, even of being myself a cause of contention, but my own relationship to Cousin Alida had been clear. She had been kind and warm and generous to me and I realized acutely that my life was going to be still more narrow without her. I reproached myself for not having gone more often to see her during the past few years.

The funeral was held at the church of St. Luke and the Epiphany on Thirteenth Street. Mother went up for it but she absolutely refused to allow me to go because of my cold. We fought about it all Wednesday and I took up the argument again at breakfast on Thursday, but she was adamant. I despised myself for not defying her and going anyhow—I was thirty-one, wasn't I?—but I did not have the courage to do it. I could not face the days of her displeasure afterwards, the accusing silence, the mournful sighs, the bitter asides about ingratitude and wilfulness. Besides, as she pointed out to me, if my cold should get worse and go into pneumonia, the burden of my illness would fall on her. The weather supported her, for it was March at its worst, gray, raw, just above freezing, with a wind like a knife.

Mother took the eleven o'clock up and would be back on the six-fifteen. It was Delia's day off; she gave me my lunch early, as she would not have dared to do had Mother been there, and went off at half past one to spend the afternoon and evening with her sister.

The house was dim and empty and, except for the wind rattling the shutters, quiet as the tomb. The mail had been brought in, the wood boxes and coal scuttles neatly filled; there was nothing more to bring Tony into the house. From the bathroom window I saw a light in the window of his room over the stable and wondered what he was doing. He was not reading, I was sure of that.

Mother had an old sealskin cape, worn to the bare skin in spots, which we kept hanging on a peg in the back entry to use when one or the other of us ran out for an errand on a cold day. Throwing it around my shoulders I went out into the yard and crossed to the stable. I had a pretext ready; I was going to ask Tony to fix the loose knob on the cellar door. It was in my mind, with timid daring, that we could chat a bit while he did it and that after he had finished I might make some tea and we might drink it together at the kitchen table. The kitchen, which Delia had left in perfect order, was a hospitable room, with the red and white checked tablecloth, the chinks of red around the stove lids on the big iron range and the kettle singing on the back of it.

Tony must have seen me coming, for he met me at the foot of his narrow, boxed-in staircase. Perhaps he had been feeling as lonely as I had.

"Miss Roberta, you are coming to see my room!" he exclaimed, with that smile of his, and led the way up the stairs. As if in a trance I followed him.

He had two rooms, a small bedroom and a slightly larger sitting room. The sitting room was heated by a small airtight stove and it was warm and cosy. The light that I had seen came from an old student lamp set on the inlaid chest of drawers that he had rescued from our attic. The sofa which he had been working on so long was finished and in place against the wall, under a picture also from the attic, an old engraving of the Washington family at Mt. Vernon framed in tarnished gilt. The easy chair, still rocking a little, which had once been painted a hideous green, was now rubbed down to its base—persimmon, I think it was. The built-in cupboard was still green. The only thing in the room that I did not recognize as being ours in another form was a string of dried red peppers hanging by the door.

"Why," I cried, "you've made a lovely room of this!"

He took off my cape and hung it on a hook behind the door and led me to the rocking chair. "Sit down, please. Now the room is perfect. It has a lady visitor."

"Oh, but I mustn't stay. I just came to—"

"But why not stay a little while? I was just fixing myself some mulled wine. You must taste it and see if you like it."

I had not noticed a little pan on the top of the stove, but now I did and the spicy fragrance that came from it. He took a bottle from the cupboard and added some red wine to what was in the pan, put in sugar, ginger, cinnamon and a clove or two, stirred the mixture with a wooden spoon.

"My friend Alf Brown showed me how to do this. It is cheerful on a dark afternoon."

I had risen from the rocking chair but he gently forced me back again, his hands firm on my shoulders.

"Sit down. Be patient. It only takes a few minutes."

I remember how his thick dark hair fell down over his forehead and I almost had to hold my hand to keep it from lifting itself to push back that lock of hair. His eyes were dark and glowing, his smile at once teasing and, almost, ardent. I felt suddenly helpless and confused and, too, happy.

He brought out two cups from the cupboard, a plain white one, thick, and one with small prim flowers on it. The Lowestoft! I thought indignantly, but as if he read my mind he disarmed me at once.

"This kitchen one Delia thinks good enough for me, and this other one I borrowed. I do not like to drink out of flowerpots, but now I will and you shall have the pretty one."

He filled both cups, gave me the Lowestoft and raised the kitchen cup. "To us!" he said.

As if mesmerized I lifted the cup to my lips and tasted it. The hot sweet spicy wine was good, and heady too. This is disgraceful, I told myself; what would Father say?—but I drank it slowly, promising myself that as soon as I had finished it I would leave. He sat down in the slat-back chair opposite me and tilted it back against the wall.

"You were feeling sad and alone? Your cousin who died, you loved her?"

"Yes, I did. Very much. She was older than Mother but in some ways she seemed much younger. At least she seemed to understand more. She was quite rich, too. That was nice."

He laughed and I laughed, feeling amazingly free and witty. He refilled my cup.

"You wanted very much to go to the funeral?"

"Yes. I thought I did. Perhaps it was mostly because Mother didn't want me to. I don't like funerals really."

"But she left you alone, your mother. You must like that once in a while. You are never alone."

That seemed to me extraordinarily perceptive of him. Though I would have liked to encourage him to enlarge on what he had noticed about me, I deemed it prudent to turn the conversation from me to him. "What were you doing before I came?"

"I was mending my sock." He gestured towards the sofa where he had tossed it with the needle still sticking in it. I reached over and picked it up.

"I'll finish it for you," I said.

He had no thimble, of course, and the thread was brown instead of black, but the hole was in the toe where it would not show anyhow. I made a neat darn that would be comfortable to walk on, while he sat watching me under his thick eyebrows.

"You have lovely hands," he said, "and your nostrils are cut like shells. But your mouth is untried. Shall I try it?"

I did not know what he meant at first, not until he bent over me, took the sock out of my hands, pulled me to my feet and kissed me. I had been kissed once before, by Ned Wadsworth. This was quite different. His lips were so sweet it surprised me. Sweet and hot like the wine.

I could have gone then. I could have broken away and run across the yard to the house. He would not have stopped me.

I stayed. The sofa was there. Perhaps I dishonored whichever of my ancestors it belonged to, but I was not thinking of that. Mother had always given me to understand that the act of love was unpleasant for a woman, that it was a duty she owed her husband, or a pleasure that he enjoyed at her expense, or a bad joke played on her by the unrelenting human instinct to reproduce. I have not found it so, either that time or later. It was Tony who tired of it, not I.

May 20th

26

I went to bed last night exhausted and drained by the attempt to go all the way in honesty. It is not easy for a woman to write out on paper, even though when it is all written she will burn it, that she loved a man and he tired of her. But perhaps it was easier to write that than to ask myself why I gave myself to him in the first place. *Gave myself*—what a conventional, pretentious phrase. Why Roberta Ewing Dobson flung herself at an Italian hired man. Because I was lonely? Because of the wine? Because of some hidden submerged unacknowledged resentment towards Mother and all she stood for? Because life was passing me by and this was my only chance? Because Tony himself was handsome and lovable? Or because of all these reasons rolled together. Probably nothing is ever simple, no motive ever unmixed. Suddenly, by chance, the circumstances, hidden forces, attractions, longings, combine at the right moment and, as temperature and moisture combine in a hay loft, spontaneous combustion takes place.

Mother often told me, and it used to infuriate and depress me, that I was more of an observer of life than a partaker in it. If it was true, and I suppose it was at that time, then it was chiefly because I had had no opportunity to be anything but an observer. Tony offered me my chance and I took it. Since that afternoon I have known many different kinds of anguish—shame, fear, grief, betrayal, searing internal division—and some kinds of joy: passion, tenderness, hope, pride, love. I have been married, delivered of a child, deserted, bereaved. I am faced now with a question few women can have been faced with: Ought I, for my child's sake, to hand him over to the woman whom my husband married, while he was still married to me?

There can be no doubt of it, I have lived and I am living now, if to feel intensely is to be alive. There are many things in the last six and a half years that I would change if I could, but even now, even knowing what I know, I would not change that day in March.

May 21st

27

A strange thing happened this morning. When Kent and I went to the post office for the first time in several days, Tillie Elder looked at me with a sort of excitement and speculation in her eyes behind her glittering spectacles. She took a letter from the pigeonhole and stood tapping it against her other hand without giving it to me.

"There's a letter for *Mr.* Morelli," she said. "Can you give me his forwarding address?"

I told Pete the other day that Tony had died and I was pretty sure he would spread the word, but nobody had said anything to me about it. I wondered whether Tillie Elder had not heard or whether she was fishing for some direct information.

"I'll take the letter," I said. "Mr. Morelli is no longer living."

"Oh, I'm sorry. I didn't know. Or at least I heard a rumor but there's been no announcement that I know of."

"No. He died in Philadelphia some time ago. I'll take care of the letter."

She turned it over in her hands as if reluctant to give it up. "It's from Italy," she said at last and pushed it under the grill. "Was he sick long?"

"No, not long. It was pneumonia. Come, Kent."

She whipped out of the post office part of the store and into the grocery, where she took a ginger cookie from a glass-topped bin and handed it to Kent.

"Here you are, kiddo," she said brightly to him and to me, over his head, "poor little fellow. How long ago did he pass away?"

"About three months. What do you say, Kent?"

Before his murmured "thank you" was fairly out of his mouth I got us out of the store. But I could imagine the comments and questions bubbling in Tillie's mind. She's not in mourning. Of course he deserted her, but wouldn't you think she'd put on black for the little boy's sake? Likely she can't afford it. But surely she's still got the clothes she wore for her mother?

The letter bore an Italian stamp and a smudged postmark. The envelope, which was of thin foreign paper, was directed to Signor Antonio Morelli in a spidery foreign hand, a feminine hand, I thought, and that of an old person. The sender had put no address on the outside. I slid it into my bag to open in private. Who, I wondered with a stir of excitement, could be writing to Tony after all these years? So far as I knew he had never while he was with us had a letter from Italy. What might it tell me about him?

Kent pulled my sleeve. "Mama, is my daddy dead?"

My mind had been so occupied with Tillie's questions and with the letter itself that I had not thought of Kent's hearing all this or of the possible effect on him. There was a time, about a year ago, when Kent questioned me over and over about his father but I had managed to satisfy him, or perhaps only to silence him, and I had thought we were over that hurdle until he should be a good deal older, when of course I should have to deal with it all over again.

"Yes, dear, he is."

"Why?"

"Why, he was very sick and he died."

I waited for him to say, "Why didn't he come home?" and wondered how I should answer, but he said instead, "Oh. Is Auntie Grace my daddy's sister?"

"No, dear, she's a sort of cousin. But she likes you to call her Auntie."

He was silent for a little while, walking soberly beside me, his face troubled. "I wish I had a daddy," he said at last.

"Yes, darling, I wish you had."

"When is Auntie Grace coming again?"

"I don't know, dear."

"I wish she'd come."

I made no answer. We had reached home. Kent brought his marble run out onto the side porch and played with it a little listlessly while I took a hairpin from my head—slovenly trick—and slit open the letter to Tony.

It was in Italian, of course. I don't know why I had thought it would be in English. All I could understand of it was *Mi caro Antonio* and the signature, *Maria Lapiro*. The name meant nothing to me. The address was 7, via Poggetti, Treviglio, which was the name of the town where he had told me he grew up. I haven't got an Italian dictionary. There are in the library a German one, a French one, a Greek and a Latin one, but no Italian dictionary.

I told myself that there was no hurry about it. When I went to Philadelphia again I could take it to the Free Library and there would be somebody there who could translate it for me or tell me where to go. Tony was dead. The letter could mean nothing to him. There was no money in it to acknowledge, no check to cash.

For an hour or more I sat there in the sunshine with the letter in my hand, wondering what it might reveal to me about Tony, until Kent came, whining, to say he was hungry and weren't we going to have any lunch. I jumped up, knowing all at once what I was going to do.

"Of course we're going to have lunch. Right away. And then we're going to hurry and get dressed and take the train to Exeter. Wouldn't you like that? Wouldn't you like a ride on the choo-choo?"

It had flashed into my mind that I could take the letter to Luigi, the Italian who has the shoe repair shop behind the courthouse, and get him to translate it for me.

For Kent's sake I made a great affair of it. We put on our best clothes—it was too warm for his Lord Fauntleroy suit but he wore his new Russian blouse—and I took him to the station on the back of my bicycle. He was immensely excited over the train ride—two stations up the line—and Exeter, after Ewingville, seemed a metropolis. From the station we went directly to Luigi's.

During the last twenty-five years quite a number of Italians have come to this part of the country; they are mostly farm workers who have settled near Vineland, where they raise grapes, sweet potatoes and berries, but recently more and more Italian peddlers have been coming through our villages and Philadelphia is full of Italian street cleaners.

Luigi, who is a quick, neat, intelligent man of about fifty, is distinctly a cut above most of the Italian immigrants, possibly because he is a Roman while they are Calabrians and Sicilians, but also because he is a prosperous tradesman. He has a very nice repair shop, clean and neat, with linoleum on the floor in the front part of it where he sells rubbers and bedroom slippers, and in the back, screened by a rank of shelves filled with neat shoeboxes, are his machine and workbench and the piles of shabby shoes that he has repaired. The place smells not unpleasantly of leather and metal, with occasional whiffs of garlic from the rooms upstairs where his family lives. I always think of Tony when I see Italians. He never had anything at all to do with his fellow immigrants. I used to think he held himself apart from them because they were all good Catholics and he had lapsed, or perhaps it was because the northern Italians seem to look down on the southern ones. In any case he had no Italian friends coming to see him, either when he lived in the house or over the stable. If it was a little unnatural it was also less embarrassing for Mother and me.

I had thought that Luigi would translate the letter for me immediately, but there were two or three people sitting on the row of chairs waiting for him to finish their shoes so that they could wear them home.

"Leave it, leave it," Luigi said impatiently. "I will do it for you tonight when my daughter comes home. She knows English better than I do. She will write it out for you."

I was disappointed but it seemed the best I could do. I went to the post office and got a stamped envelope, addressed it to myself with their scratchy pen and took it back to Luigi. I gave him fifty cents for his time. I hope it is all right and that he will do as he promised— and quickly.

After that I took Kent to the courthouse to see where his great-grandfather used to sit when he tried cases. The courtroom was empty but I could almost imagine that I still saw Grandfather sitting there dignified and important against the colonial white paneling of that once stately room. But he was gone, and the room now looked smaller and dusty; someone had dropped a candy wrapper in the aisle and a bluebottle fly buzzed drearily against one of the high windowpanes. Kent said disgustedly, "I don't think it's very interesting, Mama."

"No, it's changed. Come on, we'll take a trolley ride."

So we had a ride on the trolley car the length of Main Street and back and then we went into the drugstore for strawberry sodas. While Kent was making the straw rattle at the bottom of his empty glass, Mr. Heritage from the bank came in, white-haired, wrinkled and twinkling.

"Why, Roberta Dobson, I haven't seen you for years! Roberta Morelli, I mean. How are you? Is this your little boy?"

And so on. I've always liked Mr. Heritage. He belongs to old times. He bought a cake of Peter's chocolate for Kent just as he used to do for me when I was little. There was only one uncomfortable moment.

"That was a bad business about Morelli," he said. "Do you ever hear from him?"

"He's dead, Mr. Heritage. He died in Philadelphia three months ago of pneumonia."

"Oh. Well. Too bad. But perhaps it's for the best."

In the train on the way home Kent suddenly said, "Mama, what's for the best?"

"For the best? I don't—oh. You wouldn't understand, dear. Wait till you're a little older."

He made no answer but pulled away from me and sat looking very intently out of the window the rest of the way home.

I wonder how long it will take Luigi to translate that letter and if he will really do it and what is in it anyhow. Probably nothing at all. But why is someone writing to Tony after all these years?

May 22nd

164

28

I was sitting on the side porch this afternoon mending napkins and Kent was lying on the floor with a battered old copy of *Little Prudy* from my own childhood, "wording" me. He was getting along very well with that artless tale, when suddenly he threw the book aside, rolled over on his back and said, "Mama?"

"Yes, dear?"

"When's Auntie Grace coming again?"

I sighed. "Pick up the book, dear, if you're not going to read any more. In this house we're as polite to books as if they were people."

Obediently he put the book on the table and came to stand on the rocker of my chair and breathe down my neck.

"When?" he said coaxingly.

"I don't know, dear. If you're tired of reading why don't you get your marble run and play with it?"

"I don't wanna."

"Don't say *wanna*. I don't want to. Speak distinctly, dear."

His face darkened and I reproached myself for picking at him. Grace would be different, I am sure, more careless, happier, easier.

"Mama, I want to go see Auntie Grace at the seashore. I want to play with Helen and Johnny and Ralph."

"It's much too early. They haven't gone to the seashore yet."

"Well, later can I? Can I, Mama? Please?"

"Don't whine, Kent. How would you like to take your crayons and draw a nice picture?"

He got off the rocker with a jolt and gave a grunt that I interpreted as assent. I went into the house and got his crayons from the shelf and some paper, and he settled down more or less contentedly to drawing children at the beach. Every few minutes he brought me something to admire. A long series of scallops, he said, was waves, and considering that he has never seen the ocean I thought this was good and praised him warmly. I was congratulating myself that I had succeeded in distracting him when he said,

"Auntie Grace would like this picture, wouldn't she? I'll keep it and give it to her next time she comes."

May 23rd

29

As I look back on those years when Mother and I shut ourselves away from the world and sat up late at night, reading, I feel a sort of nostalgia for them, along with my belated disapproval. They were an escape from life, even a denial of life, but they were cosy too, in their way, and intimate. There was a deep understanding between Mother and me and a kind of unexpressed truce, as if we had agreed without words not to hurt each other by even indirect references to what was past. We were both vulnerable. If she had put a spoke in my wheel about Ned Wadsworth I had perhaps in the same sort of way prevented her from marrying the man from Cincinnati. We were two of a kind; we would not accuse each other. We were, after all, congenial companions; we enjoyed each other's company, we had our own brand of humor, we shared an understanding of the family's past and a contempt for our neighbors.

There was a certain fillip in sitting up long past midnight when all the other lights in town were out and only people up with the sick might see our lamp. The deep silence of the country town at night was broken only by an occasional cat yowling in the darkness or the distant bark of a dog. I remember fall nights especially, with the fire blazing on the hearth and a big wooden bowl of apples between us. Goodness knows we did not need anything to make us feel superior to the people around us but it did add to our pleasure, the knowledge that we alone in the village read the kind of books we read, that we were awake and roaming far afield in rich imagination while the clods about us lay snoring. In the morning we slept late to make up and sometimes people with errands came and knocked on our door, to be told by Delia that we were still asleep and she could not disturb us.

The village buzzed and criticized and our new minister on one of his parochial calls suggested that we were offending these little ones by turning the clock upside down for no good reason. Mother made short work of him.

We always had books. There was no place in Ewingville to get them, of course, and no bookstore in Exeter worthy of the name. At intervals we went up to Philadelphia and bought what we wanted. I shall never get over the delight of new books, the clean, crisp look of them, the fragrance of new ink and new paper, the promise that they hold. If it was near the end of the quarter and we were waiting for a check, we would go to the Atheneum, in which Mother had inherited a share of stock, and borrow books instead. But we always had books.

That period did not last so very long, three or four years, broken in the middle by the summer in Germany, from which we brought home a lot of paperback German books, mostly novels. I read *The First Violin*—what a story that was. Sentimental is not the word. I wallowed in it. But I couldn't read it now. Mother, being much more ambitious than I—and perhaps having a better mind, Roberta?—read Goethe and Schiller. Sometimes she would quote some high-minded sentiment from *The Sorrows of Werther* and she larded her conversation with words like *Weltschmerz* and *Schwärmerei* and, in a philosophical phase, *Ding an sich*.

It was my thirtieth birthday that ended it. Thirty is a hard milestone for a woman to reach. I felt old at twenty, pleasantly, adventurously old, but at thirty I knew doors were shutting in my face with a bang of finality. At about that time I read somewhere—and I wish I had written down over the years quotations that have seemed to me especially good, for in so much unsystematic and haphazard reading the sources of things that I want to remember get irretrievably lost—some where I read, "Books should be a means to life, not a substitute for it." It struck me almost a physical blow, and I came out of that long reading jag like a drunk getting over a—or, rather, since I really don't know anything about intoxication, like someone waking from a long, absorbing dream, with an effort pushing back the soft warm covers and stepping out into a cold gray room.

On my thirty-first birthday, when Tony came, I was ready for him.

May 27th

30

The letter from Luigi has not come. Instead I have one from Grace.

Dear Roberta:

It is nearly two months now since that day when I went to see you and made you my proposal about adopting Anthony's son, and it is more than two weeks since you came to see me.

I have seen Father Doyle again and Mr. Kirkpatrick and I have been talking it over with my parents. They all agree that we ought to have a firm decision about it as soon as possible now, so that I won't be kept dangling and miserable, and besides if it is going to be done at all it ought to be done while Kent is still small. He is growing all the time and there is no time to lose.

From the point of view of what is best for Kent, as well as for you and me, a decision ought to be reached within the next two weeks. Then he could spend the summer with me and the Gerald children at Spring Lake and go into school in the fall. That would make an easy and natural transition for him.

Father Doyle and Mr. Kirkpatrick would both be glad to talk to you about me and my character and what I could do for Kent, so I won't go into that. I'll just say that my late husband Mr. Peacock left everything to me and I would leave everything to Kent, except for token gifts to my niece and nephews. Mr. Peacock had no children of his first marriage and he had no relatives to make trouble or try to break the will. In any case, being legally adopted, Kent would be secure.

Mr. Kirkpatrick would draw up the adoption papers and you could have your own lawyer go over them, of course. I can promise you that I am prepared to yield to your wishes in every reasonable particular. I should feel that Kent's name ought to be changed to Kent Ewing Peacock, but I can't imagine that you would object to that.

I know I could give Kent a happy childhood and every advantage. I also know that you want what's best for him. I don't want to hurry you or rush you into this but there's nothing to be gained by putting it off. Nothing is going to change except that Kent is getting older all the time.

I hope with all my heart that you will say yes, but yes or no, it is time now to decide. Please let me hear from you.

Faithfully yours,
Grace G. Peacock

So there it is. Yes or no.

I would fling back the answer "No" by return mail but that I wonder if I have the right to refuse a fortune for Kent without at least taking more time to consider it, perhaps getting some advice on it. But from whom? Ned

Wadsworth? Impossible. Besides, I know already what he would say. He knows nothing of financial pressures and what they do to your point of view.

It would be a cheap, sordid thing if in the end the issue was money. I have so little and expenses are increasing; they will go on getting bigger and bigger as Kent grows up. In a case of emergency I can sell the rest of the Ewing glass and some or all of the first editions, but it would be only a stopgap.

It is three a.m. and the garden is bright in the moonlight. Somewhere a whippoorwill is calling, surely the loneliest and most haunting of all night sounds. I have been asleep, but now I am wide awake, sitting by my bedroom window with the moon and a candle to write by.

This afternoon, feeling that I had no one to turn to, I got out my Bible and read the story of Solomon and the two women who claimed the same baby. I heard the story in Sunday School when I was little, and one often comes on references to it in books, but I think this is actually the first time that I have read it for myself. It is quite a story.

First there is all the business of both women having babies within three days of each other and one woman overlying hers and suffocating it, both of them claiming the remaining child as her own, both saying, "Nay, but the living is my son, and the dead is thy son." Heartbreaking enough. Why should they think that a man, even a king, could solve it?

"And the king said, bring me a sword. And they brought a sword before the king. And the king said, Divide the living child in two, and give half to the one and half to the other."

A preposterous idea, only to be conceived by a man; any woman with half a mind could see through it.

"Then spake the woman whose the living child was unto the king, for her bowels yearned upon her son, and she said, O my Lord, give her the living child, and in no wise slay it. But the other said"—she must have been a mental defective but she was still quite possibly the real mother—"Let it be neither mine nor thine but divide it. Then the king answered and said, Give her"—this is faulty grammar; it would have got me a bad mark in English Composition in school for confusing the antecedent of a pronoun; he meant the first *her*—"Give her the living child, and in no wise slay it: she is the mother thereof."

A contrived and muddled story but the meaning is plain. The true mother is the one who cares most for the welfare of the child. The true mother is willing to yield possession of the child to another if it is for the child's good. Both women were harlots but I can't see that that makes any real contribution to the significance of the story—or rather, I do. It accounts for the absence of fathers, of course. And if they had both been respectable widows, even widows of the same man, there would probably have been families, at least on one side, to protest against so risky an experiment on the king's part. Nevertheless the story speaks to me across all these centuries. It forces me to look again at myself, at Grace. What has she to give to Kent that I have not?

I have been over and over it, drawn up lists till my brain is addled, but there is one thing that I have not included in any of them and perhaps it is the most important of all, next to the money. She could give him pride in his father, for she knew a different Tony from the one I knew. Even though she has had the shock of discovering that he already had a wife and was not really married to her, still this does not seem to have made any real difference to her love of him, perhaps because she knows that he preferred her to me. I think there must be something essentially immoral about a woman in love who knows that her love is returned; I think I could feel as she does if I were in Grace's place. Anyhow she would talk about Tony to Kent in a way that I cannot. The next best thing to having a good, living father must be having a good, dead father whom a child can love and respect and be proud of. I could try to create a picture of Tony for Kent that would be all I wish he had been, but it would be false. Ultimately the falsity would show through. As I said to Grace that first day, Tony was a liar, a bigamist and a thief. Sooner or later Kent would sense what lies underneath the surface of any bright picture I might paint for him.

What about a mother's love? Most people would say that this is the crux of the matter, that I, having borne him out of my body and my pain, love him in a way that Grace never could, that this is the most important thing for Kent to have.

A lot of sentimental tripe has been written about mother love. When you take a hard, realistic look at it, you find that it can be possessive; it is not necessarily accompanied by wisdom; it is often combined with self-interest. My own mother brought me home at sixteen to be a comfort to her when it would plainly have been better for me to finish school and get any further education that Cousin Alida was prepared to offer me. And it has crossed my mind more than once, when I have been worried about money, that my old age at any rate will be secure, for Kent by then will be grown up and able to look after me. There have been plenty of adoptive mothers who were as ready to sacrifice themselves for their children as real mothers are. In the Solomon story is is entirely possible that the woman who cried out "Give her the child" was not physically the child's mother, possible that it was the child's own mother who would rather see him dead than see some other woman get him. But it does not affect the point of the story, which is that the woman who truly loves the child is the one who is willing to give him up.

Kent is Tony's son as much as he is mine. I forget that sometimes and think of him as all Ewing—not even all or partly Dobson. Tony preferred Grace to me; Tony's son does too, now, and perhaps always will. Perhaps he has inherited whatever it is that makes one person prefer a bouncy, easy, exuberant, outgoing, overflowing affection while another might respond to a deep-buried, painful, reserved love. It is possible that such a nature as Kent's may be open to the first kind of love and not to the second, just as certain fabrics absorb one kind of dye and resist another.

Grace says that she is sure she could give Kent a happy childhood, and I believe she could. More important, she could give him an education that would make it easy for him to develop all the lovely potentialities that lie curled up in him waiting to unfold. He is a bright little boy with a quick, retentive mind, a lively imagination, a zest for new experiences, a tenacious will; he should have every possible chance to bring these flowers of his being to fruition.

Later

Having written all this and come full circle, I took my stump of a candle and went into Kent's room to look at him. He had kicked off his covers and was lying sprawled sidewise across the bed with his nightshirt rucked up under his arms and his little behind bare in the moonlight. I straightened him out, drew up the sheet—for the early morning air is cool—and lightly

175

kissed the warm hollow at the nape of his neck, all without waking him from the deep, relaxed sleep of childhood. I put firmly out of my mind the stubborn, creeping thought of the emptiness of this house without him and instead pictured a young man with Tony's good looks and Grandfather Ewing's brains, graduating from Princeton at the top of his class.

I have come down into the kitchen and I am waiting for the water to boil for coffee. I shall write today to Mr. Kirkpatrick and ask him to set a time for an appointment.

The moon is set and the Pleiades.

Don't *posture*, Roberta.

May 28th

31

I have written the letter to Mr. Kirkpatrick, sealed
and stamped it; it is ready to mail but I have not yet
taken it to the post office. I want to be quite, quite sure
before I drop it in the slot. Not that it is final; it is only a
request for an interview; but it is a first step. It is far
easier to withdraw before you have taken that first step
than afterwards, as I very well know.

It is not that I have doubts about the rightness of my
decision—my decision, that is, if all that Grace has said
is borne out by the lawyer, the priest, her family, herself
in the final transaction. In the full afternoon sun, as in
the moonlight and the dawn, it seems to me that this is
what I ought to do. What I am questioning is not the
decision itself but my own frame of mind. It is too good.

Not that I am not suffering. I am. My heart is aching
with a physical ache, as if it were really and not merely
traditionally the seat of emotion. I go through each
small action—getting Kent's breakfast, washing his face,

tying his shoes—slowly, ceremoniously, with an anguished awareness of the approaching end of these services, as if I were in the presence of death. Tears well up in my eyes and I brush them off with the back of my wrist; when he is not looking I press my clenched hand against my mouth to stifle sobs. The letter sits on the end of the mantelpiece behind the vase of pampas grass, and not for a moment do I forget that it is there; I can almost hear it ticking, like a time bomb.

But with all of this, in spite of it, I am lifted up—exaltée, the French say—by the thought of my sacrifice, as if the knowledge that I am about to tear my heart in two for the sake of my child somehow enlarged me to more than life size, made me walk more statelily, almost as if I were treading air instead of the shabby floors of this old house.

I do not trust this feeling. I have experienced it before and I have come to believe that there is something spurious about it, as if one had invested more than one had, more of altruism, of selflessness, of humility, of love, even, and were dazzled by the glory of the appearance of it, without stopping to consider whether one had the resources to make it good. As if I were the man who jumped so high he touched the sky and never came down till the fourth of July.

In spite of not sleeping the last two or three nights, in spite of my anguish, I have not been all day drained and depleted but almost buoyant instead. When Kent was playing with his horse in the garden after supper, I reread the Solomon story, and then I went on reading, dipping here and there. Everything I read seemed to confirm the belief that I have made the right decision, that my road lies straight, if sunless, before me. Blessed are they that mourn, for they shall be comforted. . . . I walk in the way of righteousness, in the midst of the paths of judgment, that I may cause those that love me to inherit substance and that I may fill their treasuries. Curiously apt, that one; I have read it several times. The poor is hated even of his own neighbor, but the rich hath many friends. . . . I will bless the Lord who hath given me counsel; yea, my reins instruct me in the night seasons. . . . Thou hast proved mine heart; thou hast visited me in the night; thou hast tried me and findest nothing; I am purposed that my mouth shall not transgress.

Once before in my life I made a sacrifice and felt as sure as I do now that I was doing the right thing. I thought that virtue carried its own reward with it, in the sense it gave me of being good and generous and devoted.

Mother and I came back from Father's funeral in the undertaker's black carriage. The house was full of relatives, the great-aunts and Father's brother and sister, whom I scarcely knew, his nephew and niece, whom I disliked, and his mother, of whom I was ashamed. The neighbors had sent in sympathetic food, a ham, several kinds of cakes and pies, I don't remember what. Dennis and Kate had an open fire going in the parlor, and the stoves in the sitting room and dining room had been started. The fragrance of coffee filled the house. Mother threw her crepe veil back from her white and ravaged face and went about among the relatives all tragic and heartbroken and beautiful, and everybody, even the most awkward, was impressed.

Uncle Harmon, who had inherited the Dobson farm, said, "Well, now, Caroline, you'll be lonely in this big house."

Mother put her arm around my waist. "Yes, I shall. But I have my little girl to comfort me."

Uncle Harmon's son, Junior, an oaf about twenty

with stick-out ears, gave what could only be called a cackle and said, "She'll be off with the fellows."

To which Mother, with suffering in her voice, replied, "Roberta will never leave me in the lurch." And I, glaring at Junior, cried, "Of course I'll never leave you."

It was a spontaneous but vague expression of love and devotion which gushed up from my sorrowing heart. I did not think then that I was promising anything so drastic as giving up school, but during the next few days I heard Mother say several times to a friend or neighbor come to pay a call of condolence, "The house is very empty now, but Roberta declares she won't leave me; she says she doesn't want to go on with school—and really I think the long trip every day was too much for her anyhow. She's not very strong. I shall be relieved not to see her come home so tired after the struggle with train and ferry and the long walk after she gets there."

I could not remember having said in so many words that I would not go back to school but I did not like to question Mother's statement before people. After it had gone unchallenged several times it seemed to take on validity, and I began to wonder if I had actually said it and had forgotten that I had.

A week or so after the funeral Mother looked up from her desk one day where she was writing notes and said, "I am writing to Cousin Alida. Are you perfectly sure, Roberta, that you are entirely satisfied about stopping school? I shouldn't want you to have any belated regrets."

"But," I blurted, "am I stopping school?"

She looked surprised. "Isn't that what you wanted?"

"I don't know. I haven't really thought about it."

A wounded expression came over her face. "I thought of course you had. I don't want you to sacrifice yourself for me, of course, unless it's what you want to do yourself."

She paused. I swallowed and tried to speak but no words came. She made as if to tear up the letter she was writing. "In that case there's no use in going on with this. I misunderstood you. But I must confess I can't help feeling a little hurt that you have let me go on thinking that I would have your help with Father's things and all the business affairs that are such a heavy burden for me—"

"But I will help—of course I will—"

"Not if your mind is all bound up in school. You wouldn't be the least bit of good. Besides, you wouldn't even be here. Never mind, you are grown up now, you must decide what is best for *you*. Just put me out of your mind altogether and concentrate on what is best for *you*—what you want to do yourself."

"Let me think it over, overnight."

"If you need to, of course."

With a sigh she put the letter away and sat there without saying anything, her elbow on the desk and her hand shielding her eyes. After a while, unable to endure the accusing silence, I tiptoed away.

All the rest of that day she was very remote and cool and sad. If I spoke to her she replied politely but briefly; otherwise she did not speak to me. Her lips hung a little open in the way they had when she was hurt, and the lower teeth showed; she sighed audibly a good deal and did not look at me. I could hardly bear it.

I had notes of condolence of my own from the girls at school, but I could not answer them because I did not know what to say about going back to school and seeing them soon. I went into the library and sat in Father's old stationary rocker, as if there might be some comfort to be got from sitting where he always sat. I thought that Father would tell me to give up school; he always gave Mother what she wanted, as if it were a sacred duty. He adored Mother, I told myself; he was gone now, so tragically and even almost young, and it was up to me to do whatever I could to make it up to her for his loss.

An hour or two before our regular bedtime, Mother said in a voice laden with fatigue and pain, "I am very tired. I think I'll go up to bed." I got up to kiss her good night but she eluded me. Without any of the usual admonitions—"Don't stay up too late"; "Be sure to turn out the lamp"—she turned and left the room, the short train of her black dress dragging behind her. I listened to her footsteps slowly toiling up the stairs, as if each step were so difficult that she could scarcely take another.

It was not long before I followed her upstairs, but already there was no light in the crack under her closed door. I undressed and went to bed but I could not sleep. Some time after midnight I got up, wrapped my down quilt around me and sat by the window which overlooked the garden with the old box, the leafless trumpet vine over the side porch and the roof of the stable beyond, all bathed in pale light from the waning November moon.

It is hard to remember now just how I came to the decision that I did, for I see myself now through veils of later knowledge, of a sympathy, at once tender and contemptuous, for the untried and malleable girl that I was and an indignation toward Mother that only came very much later in my life. I remember only that I felt a deep sense of guilt for my own selfishness and an aching compassion for Mother, so beautiful and so sad, so disappointed, so lost, so much in need of what I and I alone could give her. What I remember most clearly is that in the morning when I told her that I didn't want to go back to school, I really didn't want to, I wanted to stay with her, and we cried in each other's arms, I had this same uplifted and exalted feeling that I reluctantly find in myself now.

It lasted for days, supported no doubt by the sunshine of Mother's tender joy and gratitude. We were never so close, so loving, so happy together as we were then.

All the same, it was not the right decision, not for me and possibly not for Mother either. She was perhaps not aware then that she had used a technique with me to control me, any more than I was, but she knew it later and so did I, and the pattern then begun with so much tenderness and loving, happy sacrifice was the one we were to live by later with self-pity and resentment. It is possible that she had discovered the technique earlier and perfected it by using it with Father, but if so I did not know it then and it is beside the point now.

There must have been more involved in my decision than the glow of sacrifice. I have thought sometimes, recently, that perhaps I felt more of an outsider with the girls at school than I recognized or was willing to recognize at the time and that I seized a chance to make my escape under the most noble disguise. It is certain that I did not look squarely enough at the consequences of my generous gesture: the lost opportunities for mental development, the lost chances to meet boys, the quietness of our life in Ewingville, the deadly monotony and boredom of this small country town, the too close and sensitive interweaving of Mother's life and mine, so that her moods, her tone of voice, her scorn, her anger, had more weight with me than they should have had. It was not till much later that I realized what I had done for myself that day—and for Mother too. It cannot have been always good for her to be bound so closely with me, even if she was stronger.

I try to think how she felt, what she thought of it all. She cannot have intended what came, even though much of it was happy and we were undoubtedly congenial; we got more pleasure in each other's company than we did from that of most people outside the family. She must have slipped into it, unwittingly, propelled by her own need. She was only thirty-seven—my own age now, though she seemed so old to me, so all-wise and all-powerful.

I do not trust the moral euphoria that comes out of sacrifice. I do not want to hold on to Kent as Mother held on to me. I do not want to deceive myself. I wish my reins would instruct me in the night season.

June 5th

32

It is childish to make a sacrifice without counting the cost, without looking to see what one's life will be after the irreversible decision is made, after the glow has faded away, reaction has set in, and the future is a verdict without possibility of appeal.

I could not live in Ewingville without Kent. I could not bear the empty house. I could not look to anyone else to fill the space in my house, in my life. Except for Kent there is absolutely no one who needs me.

Even if I could shut myself up in the house with my books there would always be the village beyond my gates. If people gossiped before and condemned, that would be nothing to what they would say when they learned that I had given my son away to a woman whom nobody had ever heard of. Life in Ewingville would be intolerable, quite apart from the loneliness of my house.

The Ewings as a family would come to an end if Kent became a Peacock. He would bear the name as a middle name—or more likely an initial, Kent E. Peacock—but he would soon forget what I have told him about it and he would hear no more. He would not know that his ancestors came to South Jersey before William Penn; that they once owned thousands of acres of fields, woods and creek; that they became Episcopalians and gave the land for one of the oldest and prettiest churches in this region; that one forefather owned a factory which made glass that is still prized and another was a famous judge; that they were people who read and thought and went to plays in Philadelphia and traveled in Europe. And all these Ewing forefathers who expected their descendants to carry on something more than just their blood would be cut off, dismissed, forgotten.

All my life I have held the Ewing tradition in reverence, regarded it as a trust, a duty, a sacred charge—if I am honest, as an emblem of superiority as well. My pride has been lodged in it, my very identity inseparable from it. Yet after all I am only half Ewing; I am also half Dobson. Mother never let me forget that.

"Straighten up, Roberta, you're getting round-shouldered like your father. Step lightly. You have the Dobson heavy tread. You plant your feet down as if you were following a plow. The Dobsons have a peasant look about them; it's partly their thick shoulders, but its also in the way they plod, plod, plod. Remember the Lady of the Lake—

> "E'en the slight harebell raised its head,
> Elastic from her airy tread.

Try to walk more like Ellen. Try to make your tread more airy."

I went out into the field and practiced. We have no harebells in Ewingville but chicory was in bloom and I stepped carefully on the blue blossoms, one after another. Stiff and wiry, they sprang back again and I went home justified. The fair Ellen had nothing on me. But it stuck in my mind that the Dobsons walked like peasants. And yet I have always felt myself more Ewing than Dobson.

As to the Ewing blood, always it was diluted, in every generation when a Ewing married, but the earlier ones had married Frenches, Bairds, Moores. Even my father came wholly into the Ewing milieu. The home, the farm, the furniture, the tradition enveloped him. Kent is half Morelli, one fourth Dobson, only one fourth Ewing. I don't know how much of the Ewings is left, really, in Kent, or how much is left of any old family when its money is gone. I cannot hold on to Kent for the sake of preserving the Ewing tradition, but without him I cannot stay here and preserve it myself.

I could, I suppose, put into storage the best of the furniture and glass and books, to bequeath to Kent when I die. I could sell the house and the farm and get out. I could buy an annuity and go to Europe and live. Even with a not very large annuity I could live comfortably in that pension in Paris or with the family in Heidelberg or in the *pensione* overlooking the Arno and have all of the beauty and the culture of Europe at my doorstep.

I have seen women who lived that way. They were the mainstay of the pensions. They lived frugally but comfortably, some of them even elegantly; they belonged to the American or the English colony where they were; they went to concerts, plays, operas, tea parties, museums, picnics, excursions; they took language lessons; they never stopped learning. Mother and I used to talk about them and say how sensible they were; on incomes that would have meant poverty and dullness in America they lived delightful lives in Europe.

There might even be, some time, a widower, a little eccentric, perhaps, a retired professor most likely, but kindly and lonely, whose mind might march with mine, who might find me, with my aristocratic nose and my hair turned white, distinguished-looking.

Daydreaming again, Roberta.

June 6th

33

But if I daydream, if I find in the blank and faceless future material for daydreaming, then my renunciation is not altogether a noble sacrifice; it admits, some-where, something for me. Though I throw out the lonely professor with shame for my childishness, I can still see realistically a life that would be bearable, even pleasur-able, a freedom that I have never had. I can put my whole mind on what is best for Kent, without fearing that I could not, after it is too late, endure the conse-quences.

June 7th

34

This morning I took the letter to Mr. Kirkpatrick down from the mantelpiece, walked to the post office with it and dropped it in the slot under the little window. As it fell with a little whisper like a sigh into the box below, Tillie Elder behind the grille said,

"There's a letter for you, Roberta. It's been here three days. I was beginning to wonder if you'd gone away but Esther Snaith said she'd seen you putting out the garbage so I knew you weren't away—or sick either. It's a first class letter and it looks like your handwriting. Maybe it's just a receipt and you aren't in any hurry for it, but I like to feel that the mail's all been delivered promptly."

She sounded annoyed because I hadn't come to get it. I thanked her and took it. It was my handwriting; it was the envelope that I had given Luigi. I had forgotten all about the letter for Tony, in my mental turmoil.

At once I wanted my letter to Mr. Kirkpatrick back

again. There just might be something in the letter to Tony that would throw a new light on things. "I've changed my mind," I said to Tillie. "I don't want to mail that letter after all. Do you mind handing it back to me?"

"It's against the law," she said primly. "Once a letter's mailed it's out of the sender's hands."

"But it hasn't been postmarked yet. It's not really mailed."

Her lips were a thin, hard line. "No, I'm sorry. I really couldn't."

I knew when I was defeated and I didn't want her to think the letter was important enough to be worth steaming open to find out what was in it. I shrugged my shoulders. "Oh, well, it's immaterial, really."

But I left the post office feeling angry. Kent at my heels was demanding, "Why won't she give you the letter, Mama? Why didn't you want to mail it? Why?"

"Never mind," I snapped.

When we got home I gave him a glass of milk and a plate of sandwiches and told him to pretend he was an explorer and eat his lunch in the garden. Then I went into the dim, cool library and sat down in Father's chair and opened the letter that Luigi had sent.

The original letter to Tony was there, a little limp and stained, as if something had been spilled on it, and with it, on blue-lined tablet paper and in Luigi's daughter's public-school Spencerian hand, the translation.

My dear Antonio:

You will be surprised to hear from me after a so long silence. I often think of you; I have not forgotten you; indeed I could not forget your parents' son. But I am old now and it takes longer to do the things that used to do themselves, almost, so quickly. I spend much time sit-

ting in the sun and dozing. You will think I am very lazy and good for nothing. I do not write many letters, except to my daughter-in-law. I think you do not know that my son has died and left a widow and four children. But the eldest is almost grown now and will soon be a financial help to his mother as well as always the good son and great comfort that he is. Meanwhile I am going to sell my house in Treviglio and go to live with my daughter-in-law and my grandchildren, so that we can combine our slender resources.

It was only a rambling letter, I thought, disappointed by the letter and still ruffled from my defeat by Tillie Elder, written by a rather unhappy and unfortunate old lady who was reaching out for sympathy. And yet, I realize with a start of surprise, it was the letter of a lady. I had not thought that Tony had any friend or relative in Italy who could write such a letter. I read on with quickened interest.

What brings me to write to you now is the question of your dear parents' graves, at the end of the garden, you remember. They have been here, undisturbed and unnoticed, almost, all these years. Not entirely untended, for my husband while he lived saw that the grass was always cut and from time to time I have put flowers on them. Always in summer at the time of their deaths. But recently the stones have fallen over and though I have intended to have them straightened up I have hesitated to spend even so small an amount as would be necessary.

Now that my property is about to be sold a question arises. The man who is buying it is rather romantic; he says he does not object to having two Protestant graves at the end of his garden behind the great old olive tree, but he wants the gravestones straightened up and he

192

wants a neat little fence around them. So I am having this done and I am paying for it out of what I receive for the property. It is not very much, only two hundred lire, but I thought that you would want to know. If you are in a position to reimburse me, I am sure that you will wish to do so. If not, do not worry, but just be thankful that your dear parents' graves will again look as they should and will continue to be respected.

I should like so much to hear from you, Antonio. I remember you as a dear boy, so handsome and vigorous, and I should like to know what has become of you. I have not heard from you since you wrote me of your marriage some years ago. I hope you have been happy. Please present my compliments to your wife and believe me, always your affectionate old friend,

Maria Lapiro

So Tony *was* telling the truth.

It is clear from this letter that his parents were gentle people, greatly loved by this gentle old lady. It follows then that the rest is true, too, that his father, as he said, forsook his Church and his vows, married an English-woman, was excommunicated, died in who knows what anguish of grief, remorse or anxiety, and, denied burial in the Catholic cemetery, was laid to rest in a friendly garden. Mrs. Lapiro does not spell it all out, she did not have to, she was writing to Tony who already knew, but it is all there implied in what she does say.

All these years I have been so certain that Tony was lying. What have I done? What have I done?

June 8th

35

Ever since I read Mrs. Lapiro's letter I have felt that I was moving in the glare of a merciless light that has exposed me as I am, in all my smallness, my suspicion, my failure of trust and generosity, my naked snobbery.

Tony knew that I did not believe his story. I never made any effort to pretend that I did.

"This is a hypocritical country," he said one day, sitting in the rocking chair in the sitting room with his feet propped up on the stove. It was sleeting outside; I remember the metallic sound of the sudden rushes of ice particles against the windows. "You say everybody is the same here but they are not. You care just as much about money and social standing as Europe, though you pretend not to. The only difference is the money is real but the social standing is a fake."

I always was affronted when Tony criticized America, as if he were striking at me, myself. He did it partly to tease me; I could see his eyes gleam but still I could not stop myself from answering hotly, "That's simply not true. Look at the poor boys who have become President!

Everybody has an equal opportunity here, if they're willing to work. It's entirely different in Europe."

"That is your theory, but your practice is different. You like to talk that way, it makes you feel fine, but you despise everybody who is not a Ewing. My father was as good as a Ewing. My mother was the daughter of a canon. Not a gun, a kind of priest, like my father. You don't believe me."

"It doesn't matter what your father was. I don't care what your father was. You are you. Don't you see, Tony? That's what America is. People come here from other countries and it doesn't make any difference what they were before. Here they are accepted for what they are in themselves."

He scowled. His face could become suddenly dark and stormy, like Kent's when he is in a fury. "You don't believe me when I tell you about my family. Why don't you? I believe you. I even believe you when you tell me that Wadsworth fellow used to court you by riding on the train with you."

He got up and stamped out of the room. I heard him putting on his galoshes and coat in the hall and then the front door slammed. I was so agitated and so cross about his going out in the storm, probably to talk and drink in Homer Thorndike's shack, that I never, until now, really took it in that he was angered because I did not accept his word.

And that was not the only time. I seem to hear him again and again through the shadows of the past saying accusingly, indignantly, "You don't believe me."

What did I do to Tony? What did it mean for him to know that I did not believe what he told me, to live in an atmosphere of constant, if silent, distrust, of unexpressed condescension, unspoken belittling, implied disparagement? What daily tearing down did he experience, what constant undermining of his self-esteem? I know, because I know what Mother's steady spoken and unspoken criticism of my own lacks, her lifted eyebrows and pursed lips, did to me, I know how small, how inconsiderable, such daily attrition can make one feel.

I thought that I was sincere when I said that it made no difference, that he was himself, that I did not care who his father was. I did care. I know I did because I know that it makes a difference in the way I think of him now, that Tony was not a common workingman but came of better stock. I see by this little sneaking feeling of relief, of satisfaction, that spreads right this minute like a faint warmth through my being, that it has mattered to me. I was not being sincere; I was being condescending. I don't care who your father was, you are you, Tony. How nice of me, a Ewing, to be so generous and broad-minded.

He knew. Tony knew. He was quick in his perceptions, intuitive, sensitive.

Perhaps that is why he came to hate me, why he escaped from me, first to Homer's shack, then to Alf Brown in New York. And Alf Brown cheated and betrayed him.

Then at the end he drifted up North Broad Street and found Grace, who trusted him, who valued him for his family as well as himself, who worked with him and helped him. Who was everything that I was not—including rich. No, that is small of me. Her money was not the most important thing she had for Tony. Perhaps it was her love. Perhaps it was most of all that she believed him.

Tony was not a good man. He took Mother's money and lost it. He deserted me. He committed bigamy. But how much am I to blame? Oh, dear God, would Tony have been different if I had been different?

June 9th

36

I am a snob. Not a superior being, an ordinary snob. A snob, according to the dictionary, is a person who meanly admires material possessions and social position. I do not admire all material possessions, only those certain ones that accompany a certain kind of social position, the right kind of house and furniture, the right sort of accent and way of speaking, the right address, the right school, the right church. Even more meanly I have disdained people without these particular marks of value.

I thought myself free from false standards, felt myself actually superior even to Mother because she was so blinded by Ned Wadsworth's squeaky voice that she could not see his worth. I was pleased with myself because I told Tony that it did not matter what his father was and felt broad-minded when I said it. Even while I looked down on Grace for her high color, her showy clothes, her monstrous house, her unfashionable address,

I took honor to myself because I was able to penetrate beyond her bad style to her good heart, her generosity, her facile love. Now, seeing myself in this merciless glare, I wonder if I was not saying quietly to myself, Tony's son is of this class, he would fit into it—and rise from it, too, with the aid of Grace's material possessions.

If I have wronged Tony by my snobbery, it is too late to undo the harm now. I can rehabilitate him in my mind, raise him to equality with me in social position if not in material possessions, or degrade myself to match him, I his equal in moral shabbiness. I can, and I will, send Mrs. Lapiro the money for the graves. But whatever I think or do now, our life together is beyond my reach. It remains forever what it was, poorer in every way than the life he had with Grace.

I do not need to ask myself where I got my snobbery from. I got it from Mother and to a lesser degree from Cousin Alida. But there must have been something in me that made me predisposed to adopt their ideas and feelings as my own without question or criticism, without even examination, as if unconsciously. I took my attitude from them without looking at it because it was useful to me in some way I did not recognize; it comforted me obscurely for being homely and out of things.

Father was no snob. I almost wrote, he was no snob because he had no grounds for being one, coming as he did from the Dobson farm, but of course he might well have been, with that background, the dictionary kind of snob, admiring, meanly admiring, the wealth and station that he did not have. But I am sure, looking back at him, that he did not. He liked things for their own sake. He adored Mother because she was herself, not because she represented or even because she could give him those worldly advantages. He liked food for its flavor; terrapin and wild duck tasted no better to him because they were on the menu of the Union League in Philadelphia. He liked fishing, his ugly stationary rocker, his dreadful horse, his work, because he liked them, not because they represented something else, something abstract and superior. He had friends whom he could bring to the house to meet Mother and others he could not. "Your father's barbershop cronies," Mother used to say with very slightly raised eyebrows, or, "Your father's family." It made no difference; he liked his friends just the same and was depressed by his family, except for Uncle Harmon's daughter.

I think I recognized this reality in Father, this security in himself and his likings; it was what took me in to sit beside him when I was hurt or anxious; it was what healed and comforted me in his presence, but it never reached the level of attention with me, I never spoke of it to myself.

Perhaps I wronged Father too. I went to him in my need and he comforted me; he may have had some satisfaction out of that. But most of the time I am afraid I thought of him as a Dobson, while Mother and I were Ewings. Most of the time I found him somewhat dull; much less interesting than Mother, less important, less fun to be with. He knew, humbly, that he could not compete with Mother and I think he seldom even tried.

He did try once, and what a failure that was! It was a May Saturday, when I was eleven—twenty-six years ago. The circus had come to Philadelphia and Father had promised to take me. Why it occurred to him to ask Uncle Harmon's daughter to go with us I don't know, except that she was just about my age and I suppose he thought she didn't have much fun. I don't know, either, why Mother didn't go. Perhaps Father didn't ask her, perhaps he had wanted to have something all his own. Perhaps he did ask her and she turned him down.

Uncle Harmon put Myrtle on the morning train in Salem, in the first car, and we got on at Ewingville, with a neat box of sandwiches for our lunch. I was wearing a blue linen dress, severely plain, and a sailor hat; my hair was braided and clubbed with a bow at the back of my neck. "You look very smart," Mother said when she kissed me good-by.

My cousin Myrtle bounced up out of her seat to welcome us loudly as we entered the car. She had on a white dress made out of a sleazy silk with an enormous pink taffeta sash tied about her middle, her light brown hair had been up all night in rags and now hung in tubular curls to her shoulders, but her face was engagingly pretty, snub-nosed, wide-mouthed, freckled, with a delicate pink in her cheeks and a deep, clear, honest blue in her wide-set eyes. She was aflame with joy over the treat that her Uncle Bob was giving her.

It was Myrtle's day. Mother had trained me to a strict decorum on expeditions away from home; not to ask for anything that was not offered, not to eat food for sale at booths or pushcarts, not to raise my voice or laugh aloud in public. Myrtle did all three. She demanded to see all the sideshows; she wanted to buy food from every vendor and eat it then and there; in the big tent she laughed so loudly over the clowns and exclaimed so ecstatically over the lady in pink tights who sailed over our heads hanging upside down from a trapeze bar that everybody within hearing turned to look at her. That their glances expressed perceptible tenderness as well as amusement did nothing to ease my embarrassment—or my envy. Doggedly I was having everything that Myrtle had—the fat lady, the giant boy, the sword swallower, the cotton candy, the pink lemonade, the huge soft pretzels—but I felt the implied comparison in the public glances, realizing that it was not in my favor, and I knew that my father's indulgent chuckles were not for me. He was getting a lot more fun out of Myrtle.

On the train going home in the late afternoon even Myrtle was tired. She leaned back against Father, her dress limp and spotted, her hair out of curl—for the day was warm and humid—her mouth drooping, while I sat upright and still crisp in the corner of the opposite seat, riding backward, which did not agree with me. When we reached Ewingville Myrtle jumped up with a return of vivacity to kiss Father good-by and thank him effusively. He got out of the train first in order to help me down the steps and when his back was turned she swooped on me, her smile swiftly vanishing, pinched my arm sharply and hissed, "You *stuck-up!*"

At dinner that evening, while I was telling Mother about the day, more and more haltingly as my eyes glazed and spots swam in the periphery of my vision, suddenly I remembered the smell of the straw in the elephant tent, and before I knew what was happening the cheap candy, the chemical lemonade, the doughy pretzels, and the good home chicken sandwiches too, gushed from me, right there at the table, in a horrible fountain.

By the time she got me mopped up, undressed, bathed, dosed with aromatic spirits of ammonia and tucked into my cool-sheeted bed—all done, I realize now, with admirable dispatch and amused sympathy—Mother had the whole story, including Myrtle's final burst of spite.

Humiliated but comforted, I fell asleep before Mother's descending footsteps reached the bottom of the stairs. I never knew of course what she said to Father, but there were no more expeditions without her. I did not even see Myrtle again until the day of Father's funeral. By that time she was a student at the Normal School—she was bright—and her hair was put up on top of her head, her freckles faded, her eyes as blue and challenging as ever.

I don't know why I think of all this now, unless perhaps it is in order to avoid more probing thoughts. The mind has ways of protecting itself from too much pain.

June 10th

37

It is easy to put the blame on Mother for all of my own failures and wrong turnings. Looking back over what I have written during these weeks I am surprised to see how much submerged resentment colors what I have said and thought about her. She brought me home from school by unfair pressure, she bound me too closely to her, she undercut my self-esteem, prevented me from knowing and loving Father as I might have done, spoiled my chances with Ned Wadsworth, ruled me with her moods, imbued me with false standards, made a snob of me.

But what is the good of laying it all on her? To what court can I go to plead my case and have judgment pronounced? Who can say to me, Yes, she was wrong and you were right? When I had spoken the judge would hear her, and she would say, Roberta had only to speak out, to say how she felt. She was a drag on me and a disappointment almost from the first, but I supported her when she got pregnant and brought disgrace upon the family; it was I who trusted Tony when she was too blinded by her own pride to see what he was, when she failed him.

Mother was so pretty and so charming, so delightful to be with when she was at her best. I love to remember the good times we had, reading late at night in a snow-storm, climbing the hill to Fiesole, gasping at the colors as the sun shone through the stained glass in the Sainte Chapelle, setting our faces to the breeze as the little boat moved up the Neckar between the vineyards and fields under the brooding castle on the hill. We laughed at the same things, touched off to giggles by the ludicrous and the over-solemn, the inconsistent and the ironic. We sparked to indignation at the same offenses. Her moments of tenderness melted my heart; her discrimination in books and art formed and informed my own tastes. She played on me as a musician plays upon his instrument and I responded to her touch with the sharps and flats that she intended. The melody was of us both. It is Mother herself whom I long to hear saying, "My poor child, you have been unfairly treated; none of your misfortunes are your own fault."

She had her own scars, no doubt. Perhaps that young man in Philadelphia who flirted with her and married someone else gave her a more serious wound than she ever admitted to anyone, even to herself. Perhaps she regretted grasping at Father in her humiliation and, after she was married and bound, felt herself trapped and cheated. I don't know how much she cared for the man from Cincinnati. He was immensely taken with her, from the first moment he saw her on the boat swinging down the deck on her morning constitutional with her violet eyes shining, her cheeks rosy in the sea air, the end of her violet scarf blowing out behind her. He had intended to go on to Rome but he changed his mind and stayed in Paris as long as we were there. Every day he came and took us somewhere, conscientiously including me, though I was glum and silent company. I would have been glad to be left out of the expeditions and allowed to go off by myself, but Mother would not hear of it for a moment, being convinced that Frenchmen would have pinched me if I had gone unprotected on the wicked streets of Paris. As a matter of fact it was Mother who got pinched once when we were walking along together.

He was a widower in his sixties, the man from Cincinnati, a lawyer and well-to-do, but dried up, bald, prosy. He was also polite and generous and anxious to please, but I thought he was a deadly bore and I made fun of him. I don't know whether Mother ever seriously thought of marrying him or whether he ever proposed to her, but I thought she drooped after we parted from him and I have sometimes accused myself of having carelessly and unthinkingly disenchanted her—though I can't imagine that he would have made her happy. But perhaps I was blinded by my own possessiveness.

After I married Tony, my relationship with Mother changed. It had to, of course. Nothing remains the same for ever. Just the fact that I no longer slept in the little room opening out of hers, where we could hear each other at night, know if one or the other was restless or awake or had a nightmare. Now I was across the wide hall in the big front bedroom which had been the Judge's, sharing the Judge's big bed with Tony. I suppose Mother heard our whispers and muffled laughter or, later on, our grim silences, and wondered or drew her own conclusions.

Apart from the actual separation caused by the change in bedrooms, it was not I who made the rift between us; it was Mother who held me off, not I who lost interest in her. It was as if she were saying tacitly to me, You wanted Tony instead of me; very well, you have him; you cannot have us both. She was remote, chilly, seemingly absent-minded with me, as if she had almost forgotten that I was there.

With Tony, on the other hand, she was charming and aware, warm, playful, admiring. She planned the meals so as to have the things he liked, exclaiming over the joy of having a man to feed again. She deferred to his opinions, gave him money when he wanted it. They spent hours playing together a two-handed card game called Spite and Malice, and when I suggested a game that three could play she reminded me that I had my baby to take care of. Then began the long conferences about the business that Tony was to start and the ways and means of accomplishing it, from which I was shut out both by their absorption in each other and by my own distrust of the plan.

Once when Tony and I had quarreled because the house was cold and the baby had a runny nose and Tony had not brought up the coal from the cellar, and Tony, after ostentatiously firing up every stove in the house, flung himself out of the house and slammed the door, Mother said to me,

"That's no way to manage him, Roberta. You simply have no idea how to get along with a man. A little sugar attracts more flies than all the vinegar in the world."

I had been up with the baby the night before; I was smarting from the quarrel with Tony; my self-control splintered. I burst out at her, "*You* have plenty of sugar for him—but not for me any more. I could manage him but you cut me out with him, you deliberately take him away from me!"

"Are you complaining because I am not sweet enough to you or because I am too sweet to Tony?"

"Both!"

Her eyes had darkened and there was that almost wild look in them, white all round as a horse's eyes will look, but I was past noticing danger signals.

"Both!" I cried.

"You are very childish, as well as jealous and ungrateful. I am trying to the best of my ability to make the best of a bad situation—which, you may remember, was not of my choosing. You are married, you have a child, you have a home. I am paying for all this, in every sense of the word. What more do you want of me?"

It was a rhetorical question but I answered it. "Love," I said.

She sighed with infinite weariness. "I do love you, Roberta, but you make it very difficult."

There were other scenes as trivial and as foolish. I was all that she said I was, childish, jealous, ungrateful, difficult. I was also wounded and frantic. I hated myself.

During the year after Tony left and even more in the months after I had been to New York and found him gone, Mother and I drew closer together, but we had never again the old pleasure in each other. The baby became the focus of our lives and I, with an immense penitential effort, yielded to her wishes and judgment in regard to him. I changed his diapers and did his washing—Delia was gone by then—while Mother cuddled and played with him, decided at what time he should go to bed and when to give him syrup of figs, sang him lullabies and showed him off to the infrequent caller.

The day Mother died, when I sat beside her waiting for the undertaker to come from Exeter, I felt bowed down, beaten, flattened to the earth with grief and guilt. I shed the bitterest tears of my life; I felt knives in my heart because I had wronged her, because she was gone and I could never make it up to her. She was only fifty-six. Even though nothing of the past could be undone, she might still have had a future; she might have lived another twenty years; they might have been years of a gentle and placid joy with a devoted daughter to serve her and a handsome, bright grandson to watch grow and develop. But there I sat beside her dead body, which lay rigid and still beautiful on her bed; all that she really was, the sparkle, the fire, the laughter, the grace, were gone forever. There was no second chance. Death had said the final word.

That was nearly three years ago. I no longer feel as I did that day—fortunately, for I could not sustain such emotion and live sanely. The dead come back and tell their story, someone has said. Mother's story is a mixed one, not all the good on her side and not all the bad on mine—nor all the good on mine, either. If there were a God like the great swooping Creator of the Sistine Chapel ceiling, or if there were a Day of Judgment at the end of time, with Christ presiding over all the sinful and the innocent souls as in the vast painting on the east wall of the chapel, Mother and I would go before Him, not to accuse each other but hand in hand, our heads bowed, supporting each other in our awe and terror, suppliants both for mercy and forgiveness.

I suppose it would be the natural thing for me now, faced with this decision about Kent, to ask myself, What would Mother say? What would her advice be? But that I am not doing. This is my decision.

June 11th

38

I wonder how Father felt about us, what he thought when he saw me becoming Mother's shadow, being absorbed into her personality, overlooking him, undervaluing what he was. Perhaps he told himself that he would not make me a rag of contention between himself and Mother, to be stretched and torn by their pulling at me from one side and the other. How can I know what was in his mind? He loved me, yet he made no real effort to hold me from Mother's grasp. He let her take me from him in a hundred ways, subtle but by no means imperceptible, let her build up a wall between him and me based on the assumption that she and I were Ewings while he was an outsider. With a humility that I see now as false he must have compared his corpulence with her beauty, his dullness with her sparkle. He helped her to paint the picture of herself as the queen who reigned over our household, whose place was unquestionable, whose sacred wishes were to be tenderly and unhesitatingly fulfilled. He honored her motherhood at the expense of his fatherhood. He must have sensed, even if dimly, what he was doing, and yet he did it, and got his comfort from his work, his books, his friends. He was there if I sought him out, but he did not seek me. He opened his hands and let me go.

I see now, in a way that I have never seen before, that I am Father's child as well as Mother's. In all my searching, all my raking of the ashes, my scrutiny of myself and of Mother, perhaps I have failed to see this most obvious thing of all. Like Father, I have been ready, through false humility, to yield my child to another, and with far less excuse. I have been on the point of giving Kent over to Grace not because I love Grace (as Father loved Mother), or because she shares a right to him, but because she can give him material advantages that I can not, because she demanded him with convincing force and vitality. I have seen myself making a noble sacrifice; I even commended my own honesty when I admitted that along with the sacrifice would go an easing of responsibility and anxiety, an escape from the life I live.

In the white glare of these shafts of light that have been like searchlights picking out first this aspect of my life and than that, I see myself poised on the brink not of nobility but of betrayal. Betrayal of Kent, of myself, from, of course, what seemed the best of motives. Perhaps most of the harm we do, we ordinary people who mean well on the whole, is done unconsciously. We do not understand our deepest longings; we act under impulses we cannot name, not necessarily the ugly ones like greed or hate or malice but simply the shabby motions of ignorance, unawareness, expediency.

This child of mine and Tony's was given into my keeping. It is not relevant what Grace is or has or wants. The child was born to me. Tony left him with me without a backward glance. This is my child, not to be a comfort and joy to me, except incidentally, but to keep, to tend, to rear, one day to set free. It is not a question of material means, not even of right or wrong; it is only a question of what is. As for the money, I must trust that it will come from somewhere. It may be that we do not need all the things I think we need.

June 12th

39

The day before yesterday a letter came from Mr. Kirkpatrick suggesting that I come to his office any afternoon next week that would be convenient to me. I wrote him at once and told him that I had changed my mind, hurrying back to the post office to get it into the afternoon mail.

The letter to Grace took longer. I worked over that most of the night, trying to find a way to put it that would close the question once and for all. I can't have her bursting in here again without warning to plead her case or sending down showers of disrupting presents. She would have heard from Mr. K. that I was ready to talk with him, so that hope would have gotten a head start. I knew that I would have to be utterly convincing.

I thought of proposing a period of two years in which she should promise not to make any attempt to see Kent or me, at the end of which we might come to some sort of pleasant agreement by which she could come and go as an "aunt." But this would be only temporizing and not satisfactory to either of us. I thought of knocking her out by sheer brute force, by saying that Tony's parents were Protestants and he himself was born and reared a Protestant and I could not consent to his son's being brought up a Catholic. But this would not be true. I counted it as one of her assets that the child would have some religious training with her no matter what it was.

I read and re-read her letter, trying to find some clue as to how I could best reach her. And then it came to me clearly that what she wants, and what her family and friends want for her, perhaps most of all, is a decision, a favorable one if possible; if not, a negative one. What she can't bear is to "be kept dangling and miserable." She hopes with all her heart, she writes, that I will say yes—"but yes or no, it is time now to decide."

She is impulsive, Grace Peacock. She saw Kent and wanted him and demanded him. She did what she could —and very effectively, too—to win his heart and to overwhelm me. But having made her effort I think she will give up as abruptly. And I seem to see her family and her priest willing to support her in getting what she wants to comfort her in her sorrow, but perhaps against their better judgment; still more ready to influence her to accept a refusal and not eat her heart out with hopes and postponements. "They all agree that we ought to have a firm decision about it as soon as possible now so that I won't be kept dangling and miserable."

I wrote the letter over and over. At first I asked her not to make any further attempt to see Kent, but then I decided not even to suggest the possibility that she might. I must assume that it was not conceivable that she could think of it. I thanked her and said that though

I had for a day or two thought it possible to talk with Mr. Kirkpatrick, it had only been in order to find out more about what she thought of doing for Kent, but that when I thought more deeply I realized that whatever she might promise to do would make no difference, for I could not give him up. That he had been given into my keeping and it was my duty to do my best for him with what I had. That it was not fair to her to temporize and let her go on hoping when I knew beyond the possibility of a doubt that in the end the answer must be no.

When I took this letter to the post office Tillie Elder said archly, "You're carrying on a furious correspondence these days." I made no answer, but I think it is a disgrace that anybody so inquisitive should be in the post office.

Today is a perfect June day. Kent and I are at the farm, I in my favorite place under the white pines, Kent in the barn with the puppies. They are six weeks old and he is choosing the one he wants to take home with him. The sky is deep blue overhead with a few transparent wisps of cloud, as if a child had written them with a wet finger. Now and then a killdeer flies above, crying "Killdee! Killdee!" and I remember that day so long ago when Ned took me to see the killdeer's nest. A hen cackles in the distance. From the field where the men are working I hear an occasional shout, and near the farmhouse wrens are spilling cascades of notes as if they were pouring them out of a silver pitcher. The sun is high and its light floods the world. It bathes the fields and penetrates in bright slivers through the fragrant canopy of pine needles over my head on to the pages of my copybook.

I have brought it with me to write in in the daylight. So much of it has been written by lamplight or candle, with darkness pressing against the windows. Now that I have figuratively come into the light—since the letter to

Tony—this light that has changed all my ideas about myself, I am seeking light literally as well. I have felt naked in the revelation that has come to me; if I could I would have pulled the rags of my customary thought around me to shield me from sunburn or put on blinders to spare my eyes. But the light brings its own tolerance with it. I set out ten weeks ago in pursuit of truth, and truth is a light as well as a scalpel and a fierce wind; it reveals, it cuts, it tears away defenses, it leaves one naked but healed, shriveled but strong.

I began this notebook with the intention of using it to find out who and what I am, to learn to know myself, but it has mostly degenerated into a rag bag into which I have crammed scraps of the day's doings: Grace came, the horse came, the letter came, Kent ran away. I have not discovered much about myself, nothing that can give me any cause for congratulation, perhaps not even very much for condemnation. I am my parents' daughter, Tony's widow, Kent's mother. I have been a snob. I have been on the verge of making a great mistake and I have drawn back in time. These things I can say; they are obvious enough. Yet they are still mere surfaces that anyone can see. They are not the deepest truth about me. They are not the *me* that thinks and writes and grieves, that judges and waits. Perhaps in the end all I can really do is to ask questions. Perhaps all that I can answer is that I *am*.

It could seem that I have got nowhere at all, that I have jumped up and down in the same place. But that is not the way I feel. I feel like a traveler who has plunged through a deep river or gone through a dark tunnel and come out on the other side into sunshine, on to firm ground. A river is the better figure, for I feel—strangely, since nothing has changed—washed, refreshed, made new. I would call it a conversion if I were a religious person, if I had any sense of having been touched by the divine. And yet is not any deep meeting with oneself, any total simplification and acceptance, essentially religious? Does God have to give His name when He knocks at the door?

Kent brings me the puppy he has chosen. It is the runt of the litter and I am relieved, for perhaps the Duchamps can sell the others for a small sum. It has, Kent points out to me, very fine markings. Both eyes are ringed with black and so are the tips of the ears that flop over; it has on its back and tail some areas of gold and black; the rest of it is white. It is a round ball of fluffiness, warm and pulsing with life; its blunt baby paws are enormous in proportion to its body; when it yawns it displays a pink mouth and serrated rows of baby teeth. Set down on the pine needles it runs a few steps, upsets itself, sits down with an air of surprise and lolls out a length of pink tongue.

"He's laughing!" cries Kent. "See, Mama, he's laughing!"

He scoops up the puppy in his arms and buries his face in it. His joy is intense, awed but tender. He is suffused with it, quivering, illuminated, softened. He asks me a hundred questions about what the puppy would like. We have already prepared a box padded with an old cushion and a piece of soft blanket for the puppy to sleep in, but I haven't the least doubt that it will wind up sharing Kent's bed. This joy is quite different from his feverish delight over the rocking horse, which troubled me so much. It is as if the life in the puppy entered Kent's own life, widening and deepening his capacity for love, so that it spreads out to include me too.

"Feel him, Mama. Feel how soft he is."

I touch the puppy's muzzle and he obligingly chews my fingers.

"See, he likes you too," says Kent generously.

The chimney on the farmhouse, rebuilt and repointed, looks very substantial and fine; the fields are ready for the haying; the corn is growing in rows of small green fountains; the hops are in blossom; an air of abundance broods over the farm. The day will come, no doubt, when the Duchamps boys will demand to buy it and can be put off no longer, when I shall have to yield to them or look for other tenants, and where could I find others as good? But that thought I can shelve for the present.

We walked home in the late afternoon, carrying the puppy in the lunch basket, Kent's voice raised in ecstatic comment until at last he ran down and we trudged along in contented silence. The rocking horse has been almost forgotten; he seldom plays with it now; he has not spoken of Grace for more than two weeks; perhaps the puppy will fill his mind and heart so full that even Helen and Johnny and Ralph will find no foothold there. The sun was blazing in the long cups of the trumpet vine over the side porch; the house inside was cool and faintly musty. It seemed more than usually spacious and serene, as if it too had been conscious of the turmoil of the ten-week-long crisis now over and had sighed with relief and settled back to enjoy another century undisturbed by change.

As I came into the sitting room my eyes fell on the green china temple dog on the mantelpiece and I had a vivid memory of Ned Wadsworth standing there that day three years ago in August, turning the dog over in his hands.

"No, I can see thee can't," he said.

Strange that the memory should have come to me so freshly, so sharply, just then, like another stab of light, uncomfortable but saving. I see now what I can do, what I must do.

June 14th

217

40

I left Kent in the garden playing with his puppy, walked slowly down First Street, turned into Market and then into Main Street and came to Ned's office. The morning was warmer than yesterday was but that was not why I walked so slowly. I was seeing the village as if for the last time—the last time at any rate, if my plans mature, as a person free to walk out when she pleases in the middle of a summer morning. It looked preternaturally lovely, as a moderately pretty girl will sometimes be made beautiful on a particular day by some circumstance of light, some chance of clothing, some visitation of emotion. Here a fence had been newly whitewashed, there a lawn freshly cut; the huckster's wagon was gay with the jewel colors of spinach and peas and lettuce, of pie cherries and bunches of radishes; St. Thomas's squat limestone tower was patterned with shadows, and old Moses was trimming the grass in the graveyard with his musically whirring mower; the shade of the elms on

218

Main Street was airy and delicate; the path in front of the ice-cream parlor had been sprinkled and smelled pleasantly acrid of wet dust.

The gold letters on the window of the old brick house which Father first turned into an office building proclaimed that Edward Wadsworth sold real estate and insurance, even though some of the letters were beginning to wear off. The same old bell over the white four-paneled door clanged as I went in.

A pointed little woman whom I did not know sat in the front office where Father's Miss Aggie used to sit; she had frizzy black hair and a sharp nose and wore paper cuffs to protect her sleeves; her voice as she said, "Yes? Can I do something for you?" made me wish I had not come.

"Please tell Mr. Wadsworth that Mrs. Morelli would like to speak to him, if he is not too busy."

"I'll see if he's free. Please take a seat."

I thought I'd rather stand as she went off into what had once been the back parlor of the house and Father's office. It was all I could do not to walk out the front door and go home, but there wasn't time, for Ned had appeared and was welcoming me as if he had been sitting there for three years waiting for me to come.

"Thee remembers Sarah Barr, doesn't thee?" He indicated his secretary and of course I recognized her. She had been young when I was and had had a hard time, had been jilted or something, had gone away to the city and was now evidently back again in Ewingville. She looked older, I thought, than I did. She was much less formidable when I knew who she was.

Ned took me into the inner office, where the bay window was open on a bank of day lilies in bloom. Less tidy than in Father's day, it still had a roll-top desk piled high with papers, cabinets about the walls and bookshelves with sets of law books, insurance reports, government documents, almanacs and the like. The only things I did not recognize were a fountain of somewhat ragged Boston fern on an iron stand and in one corner of the room a child's chair with a rag doll in it.

"Sit down, Roberta. Thee been keeping pretty well? I haven't seen thee in a long time."

He drew up a chair for me, sat down himself in his swivel chair and tilted back, clasping his hands behind his head. His eyes behind his spectacles were clear gray and kind; his smile still somehow boyish. He seemed not in the least surprised to see me, or even curious as to why I had come. He simply sat there relaxed, accepting my presence.

I was too tense to yield to the atmosphere he had created. I plunged without preliminaries into my errand.

"Do the Elders still want to give up the post office?"

Abruptly he sat up straight, brought down his hands to the arms of his chair.

"I don't know. They haven't said anything to me recently, but I don't suppose anything has changed for them. Why?"

"You were kind enough to suggest nearly three years ago that I might take it if they gave it up. Kent is old enough now not to have to be watched every minute. He can read. He ought to go to school in the fall. I need to add to my income. I thought—"

"Yes, I see. Well, Roberta, I think that's very sensible of thee. Thee'd like to have it in thy house?"

"Yes. I can give up the parlor to it. It's never used now. I think you said I could draw rent from it as well as get a salary as postmistress?"

"Yes, that's right. I've got a book about it here somewhere." After some rummaging in the bookshelves he found it in the bottom drawer of his desk, a thickish volume bound in government drab. "Here it is. I knew it was here somewhere. *The Postal Laws and Regulations of the U. S. of A.*" He opened it and scanned the table of contents. "Part Two, Title Four, Post Offices and Post-masters, is what would interest thee, and not all of that; just what it says about Fourth Class Post Offices. That's what Ewingville is, a fourth class post office." His eyes twinkled. "I hope that's not too great a shock to thee. It refers to its size and the volume of mail, not the quality of the postmaster."

"From where I stand at this moment fourth class looks about right."

He turned on me a look so sober and concerned that I regretted having spoken as I did. "Is anything wrong?" he said quickly.

"Nothing more than usual. I am just seeing things I haven't seen before. Can I have this position just for asking for it—if the Elders want to give it up, that is—or must I write a letter to the President or take an examination?"

"If it were anything but fourth class thee'd have to apply to the President *and* take an examination, but fourth class postmasters are senatorial appointments. Don't thee worry about that. If thee wants it I can fix it up with Frank Townsend. Thee'd better take this manual home with thee and look it over. It's written in offi-cialese but the meaning is there if thee digs for it."

He was riffling through the pages, marking some of them with penciled lines in the margin.

"Salaries and allowances—and these pages have to do with the building itself. 'No post office to be located in a bar room'—thee needn't worry about that! But the first thing is to find out where the Elders stand. I'll go see them right away and let thee know as soon as I can.

Thee's sure thee's all right for the present? If it's a question of money for any kind of emergency I can let thee have what thee needs—without interest."

"No, but thank you, Ned. I have just come to my senses, perhaps."

My hands were trembling as I took the book from him. Perhaps that was why Ned walked part way home with me, talking about his children as we went and about his brother Tommy, who, he said, is now a professor of sociology at Earlham College in Indiana. At the corner of First and Market he left me.

"I'll go along and see the Elders now," he said. "There's just time before dinner. I have an appointment early this afternoon but I can stop in afterwards and tell thee whatever I've learned if thee'll be at home then."

When I got home I opened the book to Part II, Title IV. The bits about fourth class post offices are scattered in with the others; as Ned said, you have to dig for it. I looked at the salary first; it is based on the volume of mail and the maximum is only a thousand dollars. But the rent can go as high as four hundred, and if the postmaster supplies the boxes himself he can get a good bit for box rent, as well as commissions on money orders— though I don't suppose there are very many of them in Ewingville. Still, say, twelve hundred dollars altogether; that would make all the difference.

I read, "He is required to keep his post office at all times in such a clean and orderly condition that it may be visited by women and children and others without impropriety or embarrassment." Well, of course. But suddenly it all seemed dreary and I began to hope that the Elders might have changed their minds.

It occurred to me to look up and see if Tillie had been telling the truth when she said that she could not give me back my letter. Under Section 489 I found that by a great deal of red tape, including applications with adequate proof, a deposit, a telegram to the postmaster of the office of address, the payment of all the expenses by the sender and an account of the whole transaction sent by registered mail to the First Assistant Postmaster General, it could be done. Not worth all the trouble. But then I saw that all this was necessary only if the letter had "passed from the mailing post office." So that Tillie had no right not to give it back to me. It makes me so indignant that I am ready and eager to take the post office away from her! She's much too inquisitive anyhow. I should be an entirely different kind of postmistress.

Ned came in as he promised that he would, a little after three. Kent was lying on his stomach on the floor of the sitting room, reading *Little Prudy* aloud to his puppy, who was asleep, also on its stomach, with its legs stretched out behind, the black pads of its feet turned up in the confiding way that very young dogs have.

Ned leaned over Kent, pretending to take a penny out of his ear, and immediately both child and dog were all over him. By the time he had been detached from them again I had learned, through asides, that it was "all right," that Tillie and Earl Elder do wish to be relieved of the post office so that they can put in a line of dry goods in the store.

I took Ned into the parlor to show him how it could be altered, one of the windows on the side toward the Snaiths made into a door, the fireplace closed up and boarded over and a stove set up in winter.

"Thee's got beautiful furniture in here," he said. "It seems a pity to shut it away in a storeroom." His hand passed over the surface of the walnut lowboy, gently, as if he were caressing a living thing. "This is older than the other things. It's Queen Anne. But they're all good."

"I won't store them," I said. "I'll find somewhere else in the house for them."

"If thee ever wanted to sell any of them thee could do very well out of it. These things are coming into their own now, especially since the World's Fair. Our Chippendale chairs were exhibited there and valued at a thousand dollars apiece. But don't thee sell without consulting me. Thee could be cheated. I'd see that thee got a fair price."

"No, I won't. Thank you."

"Well, I'd better be going along. Thee think it over and let me know what thee decides and I'll get in touch with Frank at once." He turned at the front door. "Oh, I was almost forgetting. Anna said to ask thee if you wouldn't come and have supper with us one evening next week, thee and Kent."

It was the first friendly gesture from the village in a long time. "Thank you," I said. "We'd like to very much."

"Anna will be getting in touch with thee to settle on the day."

When he had gone I sat down to enjoy my parlor, which I shall soon be losing. I intended to decide where I could put the lowboy, the sofa, the table, the wing chair and the other things, but my mind wandered.

I ought to have married Ned. He is so kind and clear, solid and honest, so sunny natured. We care about many of the same things; our roots are deep in the same soil.

But if I had, I shouldn't have Kent.

June 15th

224